Clara J. Loomis

Verse and prose

Clara J. Loomis

Verse and prose

ISBN/EAN: 9783337374105

Printed in Europe, USA, Canada, Australia, Japan

Cover: Foto ©Andreas Hilbeck / pixelio.de

More available books at **www.hansebooks.com**

VERSE

AND

PROSE

BY

CLARA J. LOOMIS.

SPRINGFIELD, MASS.:
CYRUS W. ATWOOD, PRINTER.
1887.

To

Friends of the Author

A Mother

This Little Sheaf.

PREFACE.

...

It is hardly necessary to introduce, with words of mine, these fugitive writings of my daughter to the notice of those of her friends who have requested their publication. Still I ought, in the very forefront, to state that it is not without reluctance on my part that I consent to give a permanent form to thoughts that were never intended for publicity. And I have yielded to the solicitations of many friends to do so, with hope that some heart may be strengthened, some hands uplifted, some cross more easily carried after a perusal of these pages. To the many and tried friends of my daughter I entrust this little book.

C. E. Loomis.

CONTENTS.

VERSE.

1*

PROSE.

••

FRIENDLY WORDS.

Letter to a Schoolmate.

Ah, well I remember the good times past.
  When behind the same desk we played,
And the days and the weeks flew on *so* fast
  That we prized not enough, I 'm afraid ; —

How we frolicked and laughed, and, with task half
      learned,
  Reluctantly went to recite ;
And then, with a frown we knew we had earned,
  Were told, " Stay after school to-night ! "

Perhaps you will say *that 's* a slight mistake,
  But that 's nothing new for me ;
For slips of the pen and slips of the tongue
  With school girls are customary.

And those fugitive glances across the broad aisle
  That we cast when the master was out,

2

So sure we should n't be caught, all the while,
Till we heard a sly step there-a-bout.

Then the glowing descriptions of far away beaus,
That I gave to you and you to me,
Deceiving each other,—but every one knows
That never a beau had we.

But no! I 'm mistaken again, I perceive:
Only you, on the opposite side,
Saw the best looking lad. I verily believe
This fact you would now like to hide.

And Sara, our mutual hatred of him
Who the tough old Arithmetic made
Is still quite as strong—though it may be a sin
To hate a man just for his trade.

O, the many wild scrapes that together we 've had
'Neath good Mr. Barrows' gray eyes
Were enough to make most any man mad,
And such girls as we were not wise.

And still we are school girls,—and still our young
        heads
Are as brimful of nonsense as ever,
Yes, still we are young, scarce noting the treads
Of old Time, who all ties will sever.

And now I 've arrived at the foot of the page.—
　Excuse all mistakes that you see :
Remember 't is not from a wise old sage,
　But from your humble me.

At the age of fourteen years,— 1856.

The Artist Gallery.

————◆◆◆————

DURING the week of the Fair, I visited the Artist Gallery connected with it, and saw many specimens of the Fine Arts, and propose to make this the subject of my composition. I gazed on beautiful landscapes; some, copied from Nature; others, "creations of the mind." There were a number of heads, in most of which, the artists seemed to have studied to render every feature perfect. I stood before one a long time, studying the expression of the elegant eyes. It was " Beatrice Cenci, copied from the original by Guido." Who could but admire a face so beautiful, so full of lively expression? The slightly parted lips seemed ready to speak, and I fancied the tone would be one of melody, the words of love; but no, the beautiful picture spoke only with the eyes.

There was another scene that I loved to look upon. In it there were seven figures surrounding a low couch, on which lay a tiny babe; their faces were lighted up with expressions of holy delight, and their hands upraised in seeming wonder. It represented The Infant

Saviour in the manger, and they who bent over him were the good old shepherds. It was executed by Honthurst.

Many other pictures struck my attention, but I lingered longest near these.

As I stood there, surrounded by "gems of art," with bright eyes looking down upon me on every side, from the walls, I thought their authors must be *almost* inspired. Surely, Genius is a strange, wonderful gift, that God has bestowed on a few of his creatures, and their works are treasures and blessings to the whole world.

The Art of Painting may be justly styled the noblest art given to Man. The power to portray the passions of the human face in their beauty or deformity; to exhibit lifelike imitations of Nature, in her wildest and most romantic moods; to represent vivid pictures of the imagination upon canvas, is *Genius* of a high order; and they who possess this great and noble gift, are, in one sense, lifted above their fellow-beings; and a common mind, in the presence of Genius, feels its inferiority.

To music, we sometimes listen with rapture, and for a time forget all else in the delicious strains that are poured into our very souls; but when they cease, the memory of them lingers with us but a little while, and then, they are forgotten. Not so with a noble picture, in which every line glows with the spirit of the Artist. If we have any appreciation of the beautiful, the memory of such an one would not easily be defaced, and we should still view it with the mind's eye, when for years we had not beheld it in reality.

The Poet's gift we honor. As we follow him from page to page, the beauty and meaning of his thoughts gradually are revealed to our minds : but as our eyes fall upon the same scene spread upon canvas, the same story is told in a moment. There is Painting in Poetry, and there is Poetry in Painting. Though the two are intimately connected, Painting stands, yet unrivaled, above all other attainments of Man.

1856.

Shadows.

O, I LOVE the silent shadows.
   That at evening flit around,
Seeming like a host of phantoms
   Creeping o'er the moonlit ground.
How they glide along the valley,
   Through the field, and by the wood!
Here they come in friendly clusters,
   There is one in solitude.

Now, methinks they 're holding council,
   And I list, but hear no tone;
Then I watch them wreathe together,
   While the trees above do moan.
While the mystic shades are dancing
   On the moss beneath the tree,
And I yield to dreamy visions,
   Then the angels come to me.

Then a throng of heavenly seraphs
   From their home on high descend,

Breathing low, melodious music
  As they loving o'er me bend;
If they find me sighing, grieving,
  Murmuring 'gainst the Father's will,
Of my lonely, thorny pathway,
  Low they whisper: "*Peace, be still.*"

And I list their holy teachings,
  Uttered in my eager ear,
By the sweet, angelic spirits,
  That I know are hovering near.
Though I may not view their faces,
  Yet it is enough to feel
That when worn and weary-hearted,
  Heavenly messengers will heal.

Through the hazy mist of evening,
  When the moon has left the night,
And the starlight dims and flickers,
  Then they wing their upward flight,
Then I hear their fluttering garments,
  And the rushing of white wings,
And my gentle, angel guardians
  Leave me, while the night-bird sings.

Dies away their soothing music,
  Fade the shades that lie around,
Now no voice disturbs the quiet,

Now the air echoes no sound.
Now the thin, tall, ghost-like shadows
    Cease their silent, evening play,
And creep back into the forest,
    Where they hide the livelong day.

Ever, when I 'm sad and lonely,
    To the lovely glen I go,
And, reposing by the lakelet,
    Watch the shades wave to and fro.
Then the olden dreams steal o'er me,
    And from out the "better land"
Comes to soothe my troubled spirit,
    That seraphic, shining band.

Therefore do I love the shadows
    As they softly come and fall
In the vale and down the mountain,
    And upon my chamber wall;
For with them the beings beauteous
    Of the upper sphere do come,
Come to cheer the lonely-hearted,
    From their bright and blissful home.

O, when I 've grown earth-weary,
    And the soul is sick with grief,
There is nought that soothes the spirit
    Like the angels' sweet relief.

Then the heart is filled with rapture,
While unto the soul is given,
Sacred teachings, pure and holy,
That come floating down from Heaven.

February, 1857.

The Whisper.

A LOW, sweet note came floating
  On the fragrant summer breeze :
It wandered 'mong the flowers,
  And the gentle swaying trees.

Then it nearer came and nearer,
  But I could not catch the word,
For the voice was faint and timid,
  Yet the sweetest ever heard.

It came with music laden ;
  And I bowed my head to hear,—
But I lost the gentle murmur,
  Dying, ere it reached my ear.

Then methought 't was but a fancy
  Of my drowsy brain,

And while musing thus half-sleeping
It came floating back again.

Was it the brook's low ripple
   Meandering through the wood?
Or the twitter of a swallow
   Lulling her tender brood?

Again I hushed my breathing!
   For I surely knew the tone,—
And again 't was wafted by me;—
   But so quickly had it flown,

That it now seemed less familiar
   Than when first it wandered by,
'T was so very low and flute-like,
   That it seemed a simple sigh!

Then the softest of all echoes
   Bore that strangely tender strain
Back unto my eager senses,—
   For I knew 't would come again.

A wild, wild thrill of rapture
   Ran through my trembling frame,
For a presence was beside me
   That gently breathed my name.

And that soft, delicious whisper
  That was murmured unto me —
O! that sweetest of all whispers
  Was—"*Ego amo te!*"

December, 1857.

My Baby Brother.

In a lonely, quiet valley,
  Where the waters wind and flow;
Where the shadows sleep at evening,
  And the winds breathe sweet and low;

There 's a little marble headstone,
  By a tiny, mossy grave,—
'Neath it, sleeps my baby brother;
  O'er it, drooping willows wave.

But a little while he lingered,
  Ere he weary grew of Earth,—
And my beauteous, baby brother
  Sleepeth now beneath the turf.

And with sorrow I remember
  When his form, so fair and round,
Lay within a little coffin,
  Shrouded for the cold, dark ground.

Then they brought him to the valley,
  With a slow, reluctant tread.
And with one more tearful gazing
  Laid him in his earthly bed.

But my darling, only brother
  Is a holy angel now,—
And my grieving heart is lightened,—
  Humbly to the rod I bow.

There, he is a shining seraph,
  Standing by the great, white throne,—
And I only sigh to join him
  In the great All-Father's home.

1857.

Nature's Voices.

'T is the peaceful hour of twilight,
  Every bird has sought its nest,
Every creature ceased its labor,
  All the earth is hushed to rest.

List ! I hear a swell of music,
  Floating on the still night air,
From a voice, beneath the waters,
  Of your lakelet, glassy fair.

'T is the strange, enchanting music
  Of a water-nymph or sprite,
Calling forth her host of fairies
  In the harvest-moon's pale light.

Yet, another sound of music
  Falls upon the listening ear !
Sweeter than the song of mermaids
  Is that voice so low and clear.

From the barren, topmost branches
Of an aged aspen tree
Come the liquid notes of gladness
Of a mother-bird to me.

Through the boughs the wind is moaning,
Just above the nest so high,
While my soul receives the music
Of the blackbird's lullaby.

And from yonder open window,
A cricket, on the mossy sill,
Mingles its peculiar chirping
With the mournful whip-poor-will.

They are Nature's untaught minstrels
To their Maker rendering praise,
Teaching *us* a solemn lesson,
In their simple, grateful lays:

That for our God-given existence,
And the boon of Jesus' love,
We, in gratitude, should praise Him,
E'en as angels praise, above.

January, 1858.

3

The Power of Fashion.

———•◆•———

FASHION 's a theme on every tongue,
From poor man's cot to rich man's dome,
O'er all grades of men it holds a broad sway.
The wise and the simple are charmed with its lay;
Its mantle is cut for all classes to wear,
The vicious and virtuous, the homely and fair.
It shields the head senseless,—the head, too, of
    sense,—
In no station of life can we *dodge its expense.*

When the virtuous are seen in new style of dress,
Soon the vicious appear—their exterior no less
In the height of *"the Fashion."* In full robe
    and full train.
Move this and move that, each in *Fashion* the
    same.
How can we distinguish the one from the other?
O, tell me, ye wise ones—the mystery uncover!

Such a power has Dame Fashion, mankind to
    allure.
Unless you bow lowly, you 're neglected, *be sure.*

But we 've *minds* now to clothe, as bodies you see!
If we can not dress both, which shall it be ?
Shall we toil day and night; and thus be con-
    trolled
By this Empress of Fashion, this Goddess en-
    rolled ?
Or shall we first store the *Immortal* with food;
And in seeking for knowledge, thus learn to be
    good ?
Which way shall we heed ?   Our course we must
    mould !
Reveal to us, wise ones; this truth here unfold.

The Vain Search.

A MERRY child, with blue, sunny eyes,
   And delicate cheek, and golden hair,
Was chasing the yellow-winged butterflies
   That swarmed the balmy and mild summer air,
And a laugh of glee broke over his face,
   As he bounded away on the fruitless chase.

The tiny, young feet scarce touched the ground,
   And his hands were upraised to grasp the prey,
As they flitted before him, and all around,
   Behind him, beside him, then quickly away.
Yet he vainly struggled and sprang for the prize,
   They eluded him ever, those bright butterflies.

Yet one more effort he 'll make for his aim,
   And with purpose undaunted again he starts;
Still useless the effort — his luck is the same:
   When just within reach, away it darts.

His ringleted hair flies back on the wind,
    For his hat has blown off, and is left behind.

A few swift years, and the gleeful child
    Had changed to a gay, light-hearted youth,—
He forgot the sports that his boyhood beguiled,
    And had " put away childish things," in sooth.
The phantom *Happiness* now, he pursued,
    As it glided before him, so brilliant-hued.

In the dim and distant Future it lay,
    The beautiful phantom he sought to clasp.
But hard, and rugged, and rough was the way
    His feet must tread, ere the prize he grasp!
Yet his hope was bright, for his buoyant heart
    Scarce ever had known Disappointment's smart.

But when the fair vision seemed almost his own,
    His beautiful dream of Happiness, won,
And his step 'gan to quicken — behold it had flown,
    Was as distant as when the chase begun,—
And his heart sank down on the weary road,
    For " hope deferred " is a grievous load.

A span, a little space of time,
    And the hopeful youth a man was grown.
E'en now he seemed on life's decline,

For manhood's vigor and strength had flown.
Yet earthly happiness still he sought,
  Though the search with painful toil was fraught.

An old man mused on the misty Past.—
    And thought of the early race he run:
His moments now are flitting fast.
    His earthly pilgrimage well-nigh done.
But his hopes long since were raised on high,
    To Him who dwells beyond the sky.

As he sat in the summer sunlight warm.
    Where the zephyrs played with his silvery hair,
On the mossy earth knelt the aged form.
    And he whispered with trembling lips a prayer:
"O, Father, who 'st ever been kind unto me,
    Once more hear my voice, and list to my plea.

The blood in my veins is growing cold.
    My heart is chill with the frost of years,
My frame is palsied and feeble and old,
    I would linger no more in ' this vale of tears,'
Come quickly, thou angel of Death, O, come,
    And take me home—O, take me home!"

The head bent low on a pulseless breast.
    The hands hung lifeless by his side.
His plea was heard : he had gone to rest!

With a prayer on his lips, the old man died,
And the placid face a faint smile wore,
　For his soul was freed, his life-journey o'er.

And with mortal man it is ever thus!
　His search for Happiness here is vain,
Till he cross the stream that divideth us
　From the land where never is grief nor pain.
Ah, haply if he, ere the summons come,
　Hath his treasure laid in the upper home.

1858.

My Past.

—·●●·—

I HAVE come up through ranks of years,
    Which, looking backwards, I can see,
Stand with white faces wet with tears:
    And chill with sorrow seemingly,—
    I grieve not they are lost to me.

I do not gaze as they were shade,
    Formless and fashionless, but I
For each some human shape have made
    As one by one I pass them by :
    And now they haunt me mockingly.

They hold in hands as white as snow,
    Records that I have wished were dust,
So full are they of long ago ;
    Of buried faith and ruined trust :
    I would not see them, but I must.

There are no memories truly blest
    Even of those first joys I knew—

(Which being first were surely best :)
  The love I gained from the dear few,
  Of all the world most kind and true.

The hopes I built from my desire,
  Are crushed to atoms by the years:
Within my heart the living fire
  Of love, is quenched by bitter tears:
  And I crouch, slave-like, to my fears.

I dare not hope for future good,
  My past has been so desolate :
And if it should not come, or should,
  I can do nothing less than wait,
  Bowing submissive to my fate.

March, 1859.

Work and Wait.

THOUGH thy way be rough and stormy,
  And a darkened life thy fate;
Still let Faith and Hope sustain thee,
  Still, O Pilgrim! work and wait.

Ne'er was night so long and dreary,
  But the morning came at last.
Courage, then, earth-weary mortal:
  On the Lord thy burden cast.

Is thy frail heart heavy-laden,
  Dwells a grief within thy breast:
Trust this never-failing promise:
  I will give thee peace and rest!

Though afflictions sorely try thee,
  Still remember what he saith:
Happy man whom God correcteth!
  Whom he loves he chasteneth.

Yea, work on, and though he slay thee,
  Still, through all things, trust the Lord,
Wait his time, and if thou 'rt faithful
  Thou shall win the great reward.

January, 1859.

My Picture Gallery.

—•••—

NEVER ray of sunlight falls
On the high and pictured walls.
Never beam of glim'ring stars
Struggles through the window-bars.
Never silvery moonbeams fair
Light the pictures gathered there:
For this Gallery of Art,
Lieth deep within my heart.

Yet a radiance soft and clear,
Gilds each picture treasured here.
Seeming every shade to chase.
From each well-remembered face.
For 't is Memory's magic light
Resting on each figure bright;
And the faces, as I gaze.
Lead me back to other days.

O, these pictures in my heart,
Naught so beautiful in Art.

Naught in earth so dear to me,
As the vision here I see !
Here the faces of the dead
Smile upon me from o'erhead,
With the loving look of yore
That their features ever wore.

One is of a little child,
With a look so meek and mild,
And an humble, lowly air,
Such as saints are wont to wear:
Heaven's bright gates were opened wide,
When our gentle Alice died :
And an angel's crown is now
Clasped around that waxen brow.

There is one with melting eyes,
Like the blue of summer skies :
And with sunny waves of hair
Framing in a face so fair,
You can scarcely realize
She should ever utter sighs,
Or that breast should ever know
Aught of human care or woe.

But the dearest one of all,
Hanging in my Picture Hall,
Is the studious, thoughtful face

With the form of boyish grace,
With the sweet lips like a girl's,
And the soft brown eyes, and curls
With their heavy clusters now
Veiling his commanding brow.

O, his proud and lofty way!
Unto me it seems to say,
Spite of fate or destiny,
He a firm, true man will be!
Ah, that noble, glowing face,
With the form of boyish grace,
Is the dearest far to me
In my Picture Gallery.

Charity.

Be pitiful! our Father saith.
  To the weary, and the weak.
And though thy brother wandereth oft,
  And sin's dark way doth seek,
O chide him not in angry tones,
  And burning words of hate,
Nor yet in scornful silence pass,
  And leave him to his fate.

But when thou seest a brother man
  Upon the brink of shame,
Then hasten thou to his relief,
  And rescue him from blame.
And kindly take his hand in thine,
  E'en tho' 't is dipped in blood,
And tell him there is mercy still,
  If he but bow to God.

Kneel thou beside him —*plead* for him,
  To One who yet may save,—

Who e'en at the eleventh hour,
　The murderer forgave,
And melt his stony heart with love!
　He's not accursed yet!
Then tender him thy sympathy:
　His rank offense, forget.

Think that he may have striven well
　To crush the tempter down,
That when he faltered in the strife
　None helped, or cheered him on;
Think that thou mightst have fallen too,
　Had his rough path been thine —
Thy heart might now be black with guilt,
　Hardened as his by crime.

Then lift the fallen! Cheer the faint,
　The weakly ones of Earth:
And if they err, O gently chide,
　Lest they bewail their birth,
And curse the life that God bestowed,
　Or rush to him uncalled,
And meet the awful doom which on
　The unrepentant fall, —

O check the words of harsh reproof
　That passion prompts to thee.
When a frailer brother being sins,

And Christ-like thou shalt be.
If Charity doth fill thy heart,
    And pity for thy kind:
Then, when thy dying hour shall come,
    God's mercy thou wilt find.

" Be pitiful!   Be pitiful! "
    The fainting spirit cheer.
And wipe the eye and soothe the heart
    And strive to banish fear.
To him who falters by the way,
    Ere the long race is run.
Give earnest, loving words of hope.
    The goal may yet be won.

Aye! cherish Charity! and thou,
    When thy brief life is passed,
Shall enter in the golden gates.
    Be blest for aye at last :
For He who noteth all our ways
    Will, in His own good time,
Reward His faithful servants, and
    Accept them at His Shrine.

And then, O Woman! wouldst thou have
    Another bless thy name ?
Dost thou not cherish charity,
    Thine own unsullied fame ?

O, there are those in this wide world
　　Who once were pure as thou,
But, guarded not as thou hast been,
　　Are wretched outcasts now.

Mayhap an olden friend of thine,
　　Thy youthful heart's delight,
Within the tangled ways of life
　　Hath wandered from the right.
Go! Seek the fallen of thy sex
　　In Charity, not wrath:
The well-nigh ruined soul may yet
　　Return to Virtue's path.

That soul hath tasted bitterness,
　　For Vice hath left its stain,
Where Purity was once enthroned,—
　　Yet ne'er may be again.
Lest God, in tender mercy, shall
　　Send one like thee to save,
That one less mortal now may find
　　An ignominious grave.

It is thy Sister! And thy *God*
　　Has made her so to be.
Then wilt thou dare refuse the work
　　He hath appointed thee?
Let not thy worldly vanity

Obtain the triumph now :
And for thy glorious reward,
    A crown shall deck thy brow.

In which the beauteous diadem,
    Sweet Charity, shall gleam,
And be a holy emblem of
    One soul thou didst redeem
From deeper sin and darker guile,
    Ere yet it was *too late*
To turn the wayward footsteps back
    To a nobler, higher fate.

O, Charity ! Methinks *thou* art
    A " Messenger Divine."
How dost thy sacred presence make
    Our weary lives sublime ?
An angel guardian thou art,
    By God's great goodness given,
To teach men's hearts their duties here,
    To live, and act, for Heaven.

                    1857.

My Vision.

— ✦✦✦ —

I 'VE a vision now of the dreamy Past,—
   A vision of bygone years:
Which I see as a picture 's faintly seen
   Through a mist of dimming tears,
And the vision's lines seem fading in air
   As a landscape in shade appears.

I see a green vale where children play,
   And the old red school-house there,
And I hear as then the tiny bell
   Calling them in to prayer,
And the old, familiar morning song
   Floats out on the quiet air.

I 'm a child again, and I list to catch
   The fair girl teacher's tone,
Her words do yet bear goodly fruit
   From seed that then was sown,
Though she now lies sleeping, still and cold,
   In the valley green — alone.

The vision fades.   I see no more
  The children glad and gay :
No more, as when a child, with them
  I mingle in their play.
But buoyant, ardent, earnest youth
  And maidens grown, are they.

I know not where they wander now,—
  Who are living, and who are dead ;
But the gentle girl whom most I loved,
  The angels to Heaven have led.
What a strange, sad gloom came over my heart
  When they buried that beautiful head ;

With its brow as pure as the falling snow,
  And eyes of the violet's blue.
With hair like the edge of a golden cloud
  Where the sun is breaking through.
And in shade like the brown of autumn leaves,
  Or the chestnut's richer hue.

I see her as often I 've seen of old.
  How *real* doth the vision seem !
Weaving her wondrous eloquent thoughts
  Into a poet's dream,
As round her are falling the twilight shades
  And the moonlight's silvery gleam.

But other visions are rising now
  As the years go marching by,—
They are filled with a shadowy, dusky light,
  As clouds o'er a landscape lie,—
And clearer I see the forms therein
  By Memory's quickened eye.

I see in the picture that rises now
  The friends of a later time.
O, long on the pleasures of school-day scenes
  May the light of Memory shine!
How sweet in after years will seem
  The days of auld lang syne!

They are those who with me have labored long
  For the stern, hard school of life,
And now with them on the verge I stand
  Of a world of toil and strife,
And gazing into the strange beyond,
  I see it with sorrow rife.

And I turn my gaze on their faces bright:
  O what shall the future be
Of the maidens and youth who are standing now
  On the threshold of life with me?
For each must go alone — henceforth
  No teacher or guide have we.

I see, or fancy I see, far on
  Down the vista of coming years,
How each one's life is all made up
  Of mingled smiles and tears,
And their sweetest joys and fondest hopes
  Are mixed with the gloomiest fears.

Not, as their fancy had pictured them,
  A future of undimmed joy,
The consummation of all their aims,
  And pleasure with no alloy:
For rude old Time will mar their schemes,
  Or mayhap he will wholly destroy.

But one is before me now, whose brain
  Is teeming with thoughts profound,
With his noble heart and his master mind.
  He will sway the world around.
A glorious future is waiting him,
  For I see him laurel-crowned.

Now comes a fragile girl, of whom,
  Ere one brief year is fled,
If I ask of others where is she,
  They will tell me she is dead.
Disease is on her now, and Death
  Is at her vitals fed.

There 's another,—a proud, ambitious girl,
    With a high, but unworthy aim,—
The vision shows her in coming years
    As winning a glorious fame,
And as gaining by her genius rare
    The people's loud acclaim.

And her ear is charmed by the flattering song
    That ministers to her pride,
But the yearning love of her woman's heart
    Is ever unsatisfied.
O, sooner than thus pervert her powers,
    'T were better she had died.

And yet one more there is, whose aim
    Is better than all the rest.
Her only charm is a lovely soul,
    Of all sweet charms the best,
And the worthy aim of that young life
    Is to make the wretched blest.

And the coming years that maid will find
    A woman of truest worth.
Her soul is full of zeal, as she
    To her lofty task goes forth.
O, better the fame that she shall win
    Than the proudest name of Earth.

But O! that we all might take through life
  The lessons of early years,
As the chart of our earthly journeyings
  Through this weary " vale of tears."
They shall be our guide as each life-boat lone
  The shore of Eternity nears.

We shall float far apart on life's wide sea.
  Mayhap we shall ne'er meet again.
We shall see the great world, the beautiful world,
  And shall taste of its pleasure and pain :
And alas! we shall learn 't is a " Vanity Fair,"
  And its pleasures are fleeting and vain.

O then shall we turn to our long-lost youth,
  And the lessons we then were taught,
The counsels our teachers so often gave
  That with wisdom and truth were fraught,
And then shall we make them our sword and shield
  In the battle of life to be fought.

And though the ties that bind us now
  Shall ere long all be riven,
Let each one's heart and each one's life
  To noble aims be given.
Thus each one's mission all fulfilled,
  We 'll meet at last in Heaven.

1859.

Weary.

Open thy bosom, kindly Mother Earth,
  And take me in!
My frail heart faints beneath its grievous load
  Of sorrow, pain and sin.

I shrink from those stern conflicts I must wage
  In this sad life!
I shudder, knowing I must shortly go
  Into its fierce, wild strife.

O, coward heart! Be still, and suffer on,
  Nor count it loss:—
Knowest not that who would win the promised
    crown,
  First, must bear the cross!

Patience, poor heart! and in thy Father's
    strength
  Be strong and brave;
Rest, He will give thee, in His own good time;
  Rest, in the peaceful grave.

                              March 15, 1861.

Life Pictures.

————•◆•————

THROUGH windows draped in damask, and across
richly carved rosewood furniture, streamed the morning sun's golden rays, flooding the hushed apartment
with a mingled gold and crimson tinge, giving it an air
of elegance and splendor. The tall, marble statues that
smiled so grimly in the shade, and the noble paintings
on the walls, glowed with magnificence and beauty beneath the brilliant beams. But a lovelier picture was
the center-piece. In the lap of its mother lay a sleeping babe. Delicate Oriental fabrics shrouded the tiny
form, and through the gauzy drapery was dimly visible
its beautiful outline. Slowly the white lids unclosed,
and the dark, dreamy orbs were lifted to those that
gazed down upon him, brimming with a mother's tender
love. Down, down on the ruby mouth, on the snowy
brow, and on the dimpled shoulder, rained kisses, well-
ing up sweet and dewy from her grateful heart. But
the shadow of a troubled thought darkens that mother's
countenance : "The future of my child!" And clasp-

ing her jeweled hands, she sends an earnest plea upward
to the ever open ear of God,—not spoken, not whis-
pered, nor breathed, yet heard in Heaven. Let us leave
them in their luxurious home, and wait the lapse of
years.

Look! Would you know them? 'T is the same deli-
cate-featured woman, gazing from the window of a far
humbler dwelling than the first in which we met her.
She is watching the approach of a school-boy, in whose
noble countenance you may trace the beautiful babe we
beheld in its mother's arms a dozen years ago. He entered, and, tossing his books upon the table, sat down
and bowed his head upon his folded arms. "Mother, I
can 't bear it!" he exclaimed, rising impatiently, with
flashing eyes and flushed cheeks. "What, Hubert?"
she asked, and moved to the side of the troubled boy.
"Why, no one knows me now," he replied in a bitter
tone; "and the boys do n't ask me to join their plays,
and they used to think they could do nothing without
me, and I can 't study,—nor *any thing*, since father
failed and we had to come *here*," he continued, glancing
round the room scornfully. "Well, my child," spoke
the lady, calmly, "we must conquer this foolish pride:"
but her own lip trembled and her brow contracted at
the repulsive thought. He looked up in his mother's
eye, and, dropping his head in her lap, burst forth:
"Oh, mother, mother, I see,—it is just as hard for
you:" and the proud boy struggled to suppress the

choking sobs that rose in his throat. Gently she soothed
her child's wounded spirit, bidding him remember the
meek bearing of the truly good, and to aim to excel
those whose narrow minds estimate the worth of a person by external appearances. And earnestly he listened
to her loving counsel, knowing not of the effort it cost
to conceal her own emotions to speak thus hopefully:
but he went from her with a new thought in his heart,
and a deep energy to accomplish a great purpose but just
formed. He determined to rise above the level of the
companions who had withdrawn their regard for him
since their change of fortune, and in the silence of his
little room his thoughts found utterance. "A *sculptor!*
How that word thrills my inmost soul. It hath more of
music than all the world beside, and how I will toil to
win that name! I will be a slave—I will drink the bitterest dregs of the cup of Poverty,—if thus only I may
gratify this passion within, that urges me to seek the
world's applause. I see it in the future, I feel it within,
that I shall succeed. I shall grasp the laurels of renown
with eager hand and firm clutch, that my works shall
yield to me. Yes, yes, it *must* be so! I *can not* be de-
nied. *I can not die* till I see those who scorn me now,
bow in almost reverence at the shrine of the genius they
shall yet acknowledge I possess. I will remember every
mocking laugh, every bitter taunt, and *they* shall be
humbled as I have been. Then it will be *my* turn to
laugh, but I will not stoop to that. I will not con-

descend to notice even their *shame*. Ah! *how* I will
humble them!" 'T was the impetuous language of a
boy, but never forgotten. Oh, who can tell the worth of
a mother's encouraging words? What a firm, brave
spirit they infuse into a heart just ready to yield the
bright hopes and schemes that have long been cherished:
and oh, how many, whose wildest aspirations have been
realized, have attributed all their success to the influence
of a mother's tireless encouragements! Her words have
a spurring power that exerts a lasting influence on the
heart and mind of her child, and the results of her endeavors may live for ages; though *her* name be forgotten
in the great world, still the honor won by her child is
her own. Oh words! how potent they are! How may
they raise the failing courage, restore the brightest hopes,
lighten the over-burdened heart, and create affection and
gratitude in the breast of a lone earth-wanderer, or crush
the noblest aims, darken the fairest future, engender an
evil spirit, change a loving, gentle being to a hater of mankind, or blast forever the prospects of an immortal soul!

A block of Parian marble stood before him, and,
bending earnestly to the lofty task, he carved a glorious
figure. To careless eye it would seem, even now, almost
a breathing being; but to him who had toiled over the
rough stone so many days and still had but developed
the shape, it was far from being finished. With a
firm, skillful hand the deep bold lines were drawn, and
then the more delicate chiselings seemed to complete

the statue. Yet, as he walked backward and scanned
his work, his nice, discriminating eye detects a line too
faint, or the rounded outline of a limb still imperfect,
and he must retouch the work ere it is submitted to
public criticism. The arching brow is lifted slightly,
the thin nostrils rendered more transparent, the lines
about the mouth a trifle deepened, and thus the magic
hand passed over the form until a perfect figure was revealed, an *Apollo*. The sculptor gazed long and silently,
and then, sinking at the feet of his finished work, murmured: " My Mother, that thou wert here to share my
glory! but the glory of Paradise is thine. And *thou*,
the final object of my lifelong sacrifice and toils, thou
shalt go to the *World's Fair*, and bring me the palm for
which I have so long struggled. Yet who will congrat-
ulate my success?" and he sighed as he thought of his
utter loneliness.

Months passed,—slowly to the anxious sculptor, anxious and fearful for the fate of the child of his genius,—
and then came the well-earned reward. Crowds flocked
around him. The rich and gifted and renowned sought
the unknown sculptor, and his heart glowed with a laud-
able pride: his hand wrought greater wonders from the
marble, and he went bravely on in the " Battle of life."
No more suffering for the very necessities of life, no
more humbling of his proud nature; the aspirations of
his youth were fulfilled, the high aim of a lifetime ac-
complished.

Alice.

THE shadowy dimples in her cheeks,
Whene'er she smiles, whene'er she speaks,
The soft light 'mid her wavy hair,
Her white brow with no shade of care,
Her fresh girl beauty, free from art,
It was not these that stole my heart.

Nor yet the sweet, unconscious grace,
That so befits her form and face;
Nor all the gentle, winning charms
Of timid kiss and twining arms.
It was not these, my little dove,
With which you won my boyish love.

The low, sweet magic of thy tones,—
The charm most potent woman owns,—
Thy mild, persuasive, gentle word,
That e'er my better nature stirred,
Thy voice, with that low music rife,
This is my talisman through life.

A Tale of the Winds.

O, WHAT do the winds say? Is there not language in their voices? I have listened to them when they murmured in soft musical tones, when they moaned sadly as if in grief, when they whistled merrily, and when they shouted in anger, and fancied I could interpret their strange, wild language.

. The light, morning breeze strives to woo the leaves, and tells them of his home in a secluded, quiet cave far away in a beautiful valley, where he begs them to make theirs: but the leaves turn away their bright heads, while the wind sighs, and again whispers so gently and lovingly, that they can not resist his eloquence. and, bowing modestly, they consent to leave the old maple tree and go with the wind to his home. Now they are clasped in his airy. unseen arms. and away they speed over rivers and mountains and trees. leaving far behind them their native branch. till their wings grow weary, and sinking toward the earth again, they spy a little green vale, in which is a large brown rock. and beneath that is the

5

cave-home of the wind and his beautiful leaves. It is
a lonely but lovely spot: there a tiny rivulet hides its
laughing wavelets between two mossy banks; there the
willows droop and sway gracefully as the zephyr winds
round among its slight limbs, and there he will be happy,
dancing in the golden sunshine with his gay bride-leaves.
But soon their *green cheeks* are changing to the pale
brown tint of decay; their steps have ceased to fall on
the rocky floor; they have fled to a dark, gloomy corner
to die alone. The fickle wind no longer cares for them
now that they are faded, and is seeking fairer ones, who,
if they yield to his wily, flattering voice, will share the
fate of their silly sisters.

Sometimes I hear a low, mournful tone, as if some sad
heart were mourning the loss of a loved one; and listening more intently, I find it is nothing but the wind grieving over the dead flowers. Long he lingers by their little
graves, sighing that they will never again welcome his
approach; no longer they wear a deeper hue as he stoops
to kiss them; no longer their heads nod kindly, as he
fans the dew from their brows; no, they are all gone,—
withered,—dead. He will hie to his home in the leafless
woods, and wander among the trees, sadly moaning, till,
weary and lonely, his voice dies away and methinks he
sleeps.

Again, a shrill voice greets my ear. Every thing is in
motion, as the merry madcap wind comes flying over
the hills, bustling about, prying into every crevice, rat-

tling crockery, seizing caps and canes, bidding little boys
"Catch me if you can," as he trips them up, and laughing at the wrath of old bachelors, as he tips their "tiles."
O, he is a saucy, mischievous rogue, playing tricks on
every one. I never saw him with a sober visage, but
always whistling gaily, "Over the hills and far away."
Where is *his* home? O, it is any-where, every-where;
if he finds plenty of fun for himself and chagrin for his
victims, the froliesome fellow is in high glee.

Once more I hear the wind far out on the wide ocean,
and now he comes in another form. He is battling with
the furious storm-king. The dark water soon rises and
foams in great white waves. A ship is in the midst of
the two combatants. The storm-king and the hurricane together beat fiercely against the strong sides, but
neither gains the mastery. Now the wind roars fearfully, then howls like an angry demon. But the storm-king grows weak in the struggle, and the wind is conqueror. Now he tells the stately ship of his deep home
beneath the sea; and of the corals, and diamonds, and
cluster of pearls from every clime, that decorate his
princely home; and he asks the ship to go and preside
in those rich halls. But she answers: "I am bearing
precious souls across these waters, and can not sacrifice
their lives to my own happiness: then, in pity, tempt
me no longer." "Oh, come to my home, noble ship,"
spoke the wind; "thy burden of human beings will
sleep but a little while, if thou but consent. Come and

reign in those old, antique halls. There the mermaids and water nymphs flit about, twining costly gems in the carpet of sea-weed ; and there, thousands of beings are slumbering calmly." Still the good ship resisted, but the mighty wind renewed his entreaty, and the ship's heavy timbers began to creak and part asunder. Terrible shrieks fill the air. A hundred pale, frantic men are struggling in the water, in vain crying for help. They are doomed to fill "watery graves." The waves close over them, and all is calm again, on the great ocean. The wind is reveling in his deep, dark cavernhaunt, and cold corpses are strewn around him, among beautiful sea-shells and sprigs of coral. There shall they sleep "till the last trump soundeth and the sea giveth up its dead."

To a Bird

THAT FLEW IN AT THE SCHOOL-ROOM WINDOW.

O, WHEREFORE art thou here?
Bird of the forest tree, and heaven's air;
Art weary of thy flight in realms so fair,
That thou to us appear?

And wherefore doth thy wing
Thus flutter in that agitated way,
As if thy trembling spirit scarce would stay
Beneath its covering?

Dost bring sweet tales with thee
Of glories thou hast seen in earth and sky
In thy wide wanderings? Then, birdling, why
Wilt thou still silent be?

O, raise thy joyous voice,
And sing of all thy woodland mates, thy home,
And why thy wild, free spirit sought to roam,
Why this strange choice?

Where is thy native nest?
Around the foliage of some shady wood.
Where thy fond mate doth guard the tender brood
That yet in down are dressed?

Then wherefore linger thou?
Has wild ambition crept into thy heart,
And wouldst thou learning have, and bear a part
As in duties we?

A Portrait.

A LITTLE picture I will paint for you
In words, as sometimes better limners do.

A maid, just passing through a charmed door,
Childhood behind, womanhood just before :

A fawn-like manner, and a glance so shy,
I scarce can catch the color of her eye :

Sometimes, in earnest mood, I think it gray —
Calm, clear and luminous, like full-dawned day ;

And sometimes, when the gentle heart looks through,
I know it for a tender, heavenly blue :

And shady hair, but whether loosened tress,
Or band, or braid, or curl, I can not guess.

Yet this I know : somehow it lends her face
An all unstudied, yet artistic grace :

And her complexion, whether dusk or fair,
I ken not, but it suiteth well her hair:

I know it is ethereal, saintly, pure,
Like one who owns a spirit brave t' endure:

Transparent, too, as tho' her darkest thought
She need not shun, if into strong light brought:

Clouding and brightening with each emotion,
As winds will change the surface of the ocean;

And always, whether grave or glad, there sits
The signet of God's peace upon her lips.

Whate'er her dress or ornament may be,
Her robes are always white to me.

Like one who, though he treads a world all vile,
Yet keeps his spirit-raiment free from guile.

I think she hath no jewels save that one
Which we were bidden to wear by God's own Son—

The " meek and quiet spirit," that I know
She weareth always with her robe of snow.

A shrinking, sensitive, and fragile flower,
Yet strong, heroic, grand in moral power.

And much of trouble hath this young girl known.
(Perchance from it she gained her life's high tone) :

Home, friends, and careful nurture, once had she,
In a far tropic island of the sea ;

But soon a strange, inexorable fate
Cast her an orphan, poor and desolate,

On a strange shore.   Or was it Providence,
Inscrutable, yet kind, with wise intents,

Sought thus to noble ends her life to mould,
Thus cleansed from dross, developed thus the gold,

And by a stern and better discipline,
Brought strongly outward what was best within ?

O, who would dare to court the dread ordeal
Of sacrifice and loss she yet doth feel ?

Yet who but envies her the chastened will,
That calm and holy trust through good or ill,

That sweet, assured reliance on the Heart
Divine, yet human, that hath known Life's smart ?

I promised you a sketch sometime ago,
A faint, imperfect outline this, I know ;

And could I dip my pen in Heaven's light,
My picture should be fitter for your sight.

A Little Man.

———•••———

HE was a common little lad,
　Unprepossessing quite:
An unkempt look he always had,
　Repellant to the sight:
No outward power to win had he,
Child of neglect and poverty.

And worse—he had, we used to say,
　A somewhat sluggish mind,
That seemed to darkly grope its way,—
　The patient, plodding kind:
Still, with his grim persistency,
A decent scholar yet might be.

It chanced there came a holiday:
　Next morn he'd disappeared.
"Johnnie got hurted yesterday,"
　An urchin volunteered:
"We's playing on the railroad track;
There came a car along ker smack!

" And run right over Johnnie's foot.
  I hollered then, like mad :
'Cause, when I see the bloody boot.
  I knew 't was pooty bad :
And then some men, they took him home.
And sent for Dr. Morse to come,"

No small delinquents stayed that day :
  The laggards all dismissed.
The lads commanded straight away,
  The last wee lassie kissed,
I hurried through the noontide glare.
To Johnnie, propped in rocking chair :

Across another broken one
  The poor, crushed member lay :
The injured child was all alone,
  Save for the babe at play,
Soiled and untended, on the floor,
An infant two years old or more.

The mother, in some washing tub.
  Her tears that day let fall :
The father gone — a rich man's " sub."—
  To serve his country's call :
For labor is the price of bread.
And little children must be fed.

" Poor little man ! how hard it is ! "
    And then I quite broke down.
" O, yes ! do n't cry, I beg you, miss ! "
    (Said with a smothered groan) ;
" But when it 's more than I can bear,
    I try to say a little prayer :

" And then I think of what I learnéd
    Out of our reading-book,
About a man who always turned
    To good " (and here he shook
With pain, and was a moment dumb),
" Just every thing that chanced to come."

" ' If John was afflicted with sickness or pain,
    He wished himself better, but did not complain,
Nor lie down and fret in despondence and sorrow,
But said that he hoped to be better to-morrow.' "

Brave heart ! and true philosophy !
    That canceled half the sting,
Extracting, like the honey bee,
    Sweetness from every thing.
The teacher something learned, that day.
From humble little John O'Shea.

Three Curls.

HE held them up before me—three long, bright
  · rings of hair;
No word he spoke, and I was mute, as we stood
  sadly there;
Three brown and shining curls they were, a glint-
  ing in the sun.
What language had those voiceless things of our
  beloved one?
O, how the memories olden thronged in upon the
  brain!
But all their garnered sweetness, was turned to
  bitter pain
When I thought, but *this* is left us—but this,
  and nothing more—
This clustered hair, to tell of all the happiness of
  yore.

We loved her! oh we loved her—and we never
  knew how well
Till the grim phantom shade of Death across our
  threshold fell.

And passionate and pleading prayers from break-
    ing hearts put up
Might not remove the specter shade, nor stay the
    bitter cup.
I see her — not as erst I saw, flower-crowned,
    white-robed, a fair and gentle bride,
Beside the one whose manly heart throbbed high
    with love and pride,
Where music swelled, and laugh and song and
    many a merry word
Fell gayly from young, ruby lips, and naught but
    joy was heard.
While summer skies and airs were sweet, before
    June roses fled,
A message came with suddenness — a word that
    she lay dead.

Not dead! Our bright one is not dead, but passed
    from death to life!
Passed from this land of change and gloom,
      To one with glories rife!
Such beatific glories as our weak minds have not
    dreamed,
For mortal fancy may not paint the joys of the
    redeemed.
But she, with finer, subtler ear than our dull,
    earthly sense,

Had caught the Father's high command : " My
    daughter, hasten thence ! "
From o'er the crystal battlements she heard the
    angel's call :
Our tear-dimmed, straining eyes saw not beyond
    the jasper wall.

She knew the burst of melody through all that
    seraph throng.—
We caught no faintest echo from that triumphant
    song :
We only stood and wept beside her beautiful,
    cold clay.
While the pure spirit, glad and free, went on its
    shining way :
The glory of young Motherhood, that would have
    crowned her brow,
Put off for amaranthine blooms, she weareth
    sweetly now :
No taint of Earth upon her robes, in Jesus' blood
    made white :
No pain, nor sin, nor sorrow, in that land of life
    and light.

O, anguish-riven hearts, be still ! It is the
    Father's hand.
Though crushed and bleeding now ye lie, and
    can not understand

His dark, mysterious Providence, be sure He
loveth yet

The children whom He chasteneth, nor will their
woe forget.

Bless God, the tender life she gave, in yielding up
her own.

Remains to fill the aching heart, and cheer the
saddened home.

A precious, holy legacy! O, God will love to
bless

Our pure and sainted Tilla's child—the little
Motherless.

I see her now,—O, not as then; that vision
passed; but this

Not time nor change shall e'er dispel, for 't is
eternal bliss!

She wanders 'neath the Tree of Life, in that
celestial home,

And the radiance that enfolds her, is from the
great white throne.

Dear Lord! Forgive th' unchastened will, and
bid our murmuring cease.

Upon the sorely stricken hearts breathe thou the
balm of Peace!

Those soft, brown curls—he laid them back with
rev'rent, tender hand,

And slow he spoke: "I can not wish her back to
      this sad land."
Heavenward we turn our wistful eyes, and still
      Thy love I see,
For all our bitter discipline shall lead us up to
      Thee.

July, 1865.

6

On the Sea.

On the waters, mild and wide,
    My brothers sail to-day,
And o'er the rocking vessel's side
    They watch the mad waves play :
The mad and merry waters,
    The laughing, treacherous sea —
O, I would my bonnie laddies
    Were safe at home with me!
And now I mind me of an olden time,
And childish visions of a sunnier clime,
When the South land an El Dorado seemed,
And bore a part in all they planned, and dreamed,
Poring thro' long, long days o'er old romance,
Full of adventures strange, and quaint sweet fancies :
And wanderings of brave knights in distant land,
Thus, their ambitions stirred, they 've slipt from
    our fond hands.
        O angry Sea,
        Be still, be still !
And curb your passionate, stormy will;

O, beautiful, mocking, smiling Sea,
Be true to the trust I give to thee!
Pale stars in the vaulted sky,
   Golden jewels set in black,
Watch the lonely vessel fly
   On her phosphorescent track.
Hark! The sweet-toned chapel bell
Calls from cloister and from cell.
Brothers mine! our prayers ascending
May perchance with thine be blending.
   Ave Marie! Guard them well!

No more we'll roam together,
   My merry boys and I.
O'er hill, and crag, and heather,
   As in the years gone by.
I see the youthful trio,
   As in those charméd days
Thro' the old scenes they're flitting
   Across my mental gaze —
Through woody dell, and forest crypt,
All the tender foliage tipped
   With the sunlight's paling gold,
All the mellow landscape spreading
   Like a picture rare and old:
While our feet the paths are treading,
As we drove the cattle and the lambkins from the
   wold,

On the Sea they ride to-night,
The ravenous, greedy Sea,
And fast the leagues do multiply
That lie 'twixt them and me,
O, for the weird gift of a Sybil,
Their future to foretell!
Still I can pray, as they speed on the way,
Sweet Marie! Guard them well!
Full many a cycling year will find its grave,
Ere they recross the heaving, trackless wave;
Yet *sometime,* Hope will sing, my brothers twain
Shall gather 'neath the roof-tree once again.
On land or Sea,
O, hear our plea!
Still, wherever my dear ones dwell,
Ave Marie! Guard them well!

To à Picture of Virgil's Sybil.

— ◆◆◆ ——

BEAUTIFUL Sybil! With thy prophet eyes,
Canst read my horoscope in yonder skies?
Canst solve the future, that to me is sealed?
O wave thy wand, and let it be revealed!

O draw the veil, and grant me one swift look
Into the mysteries of that wonderous book!
For those deep eyes, so searching and so strange,
Seem to look *through* whate'er is in thy range.

.

Upon thy dark and splendid gypsy face
Prints of a strange and mystic power I trace:
O that those perfect lips would part and tell
What thou dost read among the stars so well!

The turbaned brow, half lost in softest shade:
The deep, warm, flesh tints, all so skillful made;
The pink flush mantling on the oval cheek,—
All, all *so* lifelike, surely sh · *must* speak!

Speak, Sybil: tell me what those glorious eyes,
With their strange light, so wonderous and so
    wise,
See 'mong the stars: thy visions there relate,
Beautiful Oracle!   O tell my fate!

Lottie.

MAKE room, sweet flowers, in your autumn bed,
For the graceful blossom we loved is dead.
All vainly we cherished her fading bloom,
Our bright one slumbers ; sweet flowers, make room.

Dear Mother Earth ! on your fragrant breast,
Make room for the tired child seeking rest !
Life's strange mosaic of joys and woes
Is finished,—and calm be her last repose !

All hushed and soothed is the turmoil now ;
All care lines fade from the fair girl brow ;
No sin, no anguish, no throb of pain,
Shall ever stir the still heart again.

On the sunny hill-slope, where soft winds blow,
Where winter skies sift their purest snow,
Where spring's first violet breath is shed,
Make room for our beautiful, holy dead.

O shining seraph at Heaven's gates.
Fling wide your portal for one who waits,
Bought with a price, and redeemed from sin !
Make room, for the white soul entering in,

Make room, sweet angels; amid your choir.
Our darling's fingers shall sweep a lyre.
The sweet voice silent shall yonder rise.
And echo the anthems of Paradise.

Dear Jesus. when we, too, trembling, come
To the River's brink,—oh then, make room,
Make room for us all, on the Heart Divine.
Where Lottie is folded forever thine.

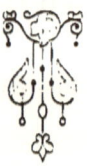

Spring.

⸺ ･●● ⸺

I know where the flowers are springing :
  I know where the brooks are free :
I know where the birds are singing
  A jubilant welcome for me.
Yet brown and crisp is the heather :
  Yet bare are the forest trees ;
And something of wintery weather
  Lingereth yet in the breeze.

But the dear old hills are calling,
  And O! how I long to respond!
For the genial showers are falling
  On the wood and meadow beyond.
I know what to seek in the woodland :
  The trailing arbutus is there :
And down in the meadow the cowslip
  Is dressing her bright yellow hair.

And innocence, pale and saintly,
  And passionless violets white,

Breathe over the marsh so faintly,
   As they wake from the long winter night.
By and by, the gay cardinal flower
   Will flash out her glowing red,
With the leaves of a wild-wood bower
   All over her blushes spread.

O, I hear you, my fair, dainty beauties —
   Your perfumed, but voiceless call!
So I 'll hie me away from all duties,
   And hasten to welcome ye all.
Yes, welcome the Spring, and the gladness
   Of quickening sunshine and rain;
She poureth a sweet, subtle madness
   Through Nature's every vein.

So, while the soft zephyrs are wooing
   My senses, with lover-like art,
I 'll follow where songsters are cooing,
   And blossoms spring up from earth's heart,
And wand'ring in fields fresh and vernal,
   I 'll dream of the glorious home
Where beauty and Spring are eternal,
   And winter and Death never come.

A Voice from the Children.

O, LOVE us, dear big people! It is the children's
    cry.
Life is a strange, hard problem we 've just began to
    try;
We do not understand it, and only this we know;
O love us, do but love us, for that will help us so.

Our minds are very little; our years are very few.
Do you guess the questioning glances we upward
    turn to you?
Do you know how hard we struggle with all our
    feeble might?
How we grope to find your Jesus? how we want to
    do the right?
'T is but a sorry struggle we make of it, 't is true;
And so, you dear big people, we turn for help to
    you;
Our intellects are young, our faculties are small,
Yet in our yearning bosoms we 've heard the
    Saviour's call.

O, often in our playing we 've felt our need of
   Him ;
It is a sacred feeling, and not a childish whim ;
'T is not a morbid notion, and not a vain desire
Should thus, with holy longings, our little hearts
   inspire.

O, at the solemn nightfall, after our prayer and
   song,
We grievingly remember how often we 've done
   wrong,
And scarcely dare to slumber when the lamp is
   ta'en away :
But O, good Christian people, you 've learned a
   better way.

You 've learned to keep from sinning, and God's
   sweet favor thus
Abideth ever with you. — O tell it unto us,
The secret of your living — that something you call
   Faith,
That saves you from transgression, and from the
   second death.

Teach us that precious lesson ; we will not slight
   the task ;
Show us the way to Jesus ; love us ; 't is all we
   ask ;

Our little feet may stumble, and perchance may
    wander far.
But cherish us. and love us. and be our guiding
    star.

From mouths of babes and sucklings He has per-
    fected praise !
O. in that grand. sweet anthem. which angel chil-
    dren raise.
We long to join our voices. and honor Jesus. too.
Did he not bid us welcome ? O, then. why will not
    you ?

" You think we shall know better our own minds
    by-and-by ? "
Meantime we may be learning to cheat. and swear.
    and lie :
O father. mother. teacher, help us, and you shall see
What earnest little Christians even your babes may
    be.

Give us your warm. sweet sympathy, and hold us by
    the hand :
Guide us with loving patience up toward the better
    land :
Then say with full assurance there. in eternity :
Here, Lord. am I, Thy servant. with them Thou
    gavest me.

Beautiful Hands.

DIMPLED and soft, and tiny and white.
And shapely, the hands I beheld to-night.
Fluttering over piano keys
Like lilies flirting with summer breeze ;
Clasped by chivalrous young gallants
In the change of the undulating dance ;
Over them passionate vows were said
When the midnight and morning hours were
      wed ;
Dear little morsel of a hand,
Potent as witches' magic wand !

Fair, cunning fingers, dainty as snow,
How to ensnare right well you know ;
How to be graceful and busy, too,
With a charming air of "nothing to do !"
Idle as lovely, aimless as fair.
Verily ye are a pretty pair ;
Hands that were given to cheer and bless.

Folded in beautiful uselessness:
Yet Canova marble's purity
Scarce in its snow can rival thee!

Brown and bony, and wrinkled and thin,
No fairy softness nor satin-smooth skin,—
Such are another pair I know,
Warmly welcomed wherever they go,
Bearing sweet bounty to poverty's door,
Full of alms-deeds for the sick and poor;
On the brow that is wearied overmuch,
Tender and motherly fond, their touch
Falls with a gentle and restful calm,
Grateful as incense, healing as balm.

Faithful, unwearied, and cheerily too,
Doing with might what they find to do,—
Often a thankless and toilsome lot,
Unacknowledged and quite forgot:
Kind and patient, and diligent still,
Always through goodly report or ill;
These are the hands all calloused and brown,
That empty and useless never hang down.
Ah, where the vigilant Master stands,
Which will be reckoned as beautiful hands?

Insane.

THE BRIDE OF DUKE ALEXIS.

SHE sits by the turret window,
  Just as she sat of yore,
Looking away to the Southward,
  For one who will come no more.

Eagerly, vainly, watching,
  With her strained, expectant eyes,
And she sees in the far, dim distance
  A cloud of dust arise.

She thinks 't is the gallant horseman
  Coming again at last,
Riding the same black charger,
  That he rode in the distant Past.

Adown the carved old staircase,
  She glides with wingèd feet,
And heart in a sweet, wild tumult,
  The horseman brave to meet.

And lo! she finds 't is another,
  Who has ridden swiftly by —
And she goes back to her watching,
  By the casement lone and high.

The peasantry in the valley
  Know well the lady's face ;
They have seen it in the tower,
  Always in the self-same place.

And strangers. who glance at the window,
  Will turn and look up again,
To see what vision smote them
  With that sudden throb of pain.

They turn with questioning wonder,
  And see with a quick surprise,
That there dwells no light of reason
  In the depths of her mournful eyes.

The servants speak to her softly,
  In that old baronial place ;
They know every shade that crosses
  The gentle maniac's face.

And her father, the sad old Baron,
  With frantic love has sought

7

To restore to its throne — but vainly —
　　The poor mind, so distraught.

And all, with a tender reverence,
　　A loving, pitiful care,
Seek gently to draw the mad girl,
　　From her sorrowful vigil there.

But ever at hour of twilight,
　　And when the moon is high,
And oft till the dawn of morning,
　　Whoever is passing by

Still sees at the turret window,
　　What many have seen before,
A woman who looks to the Southward,
　　For one who will come no more.

The Consequences

OF

A SIXTH SENSE.

———•◦•———

I HAD been studying the chapter on the senses in
Mental Philosophy, until late in the evening, but gradually an irresistible drowsiness stole over me, and I laid
my head in the open book, and was soon roving in the
land of dreams.   And as I dreamed, I grew discontented
that we had only five senses, and murmured against the
good Father, saying: " Now, when God made us, he
might just as well have given one more, and it would
have been such a great advantage to us.   Now, if we
had the gift of second sight, how much more knowledge
we could acquire, how much easier, and then we should
be so much happier!"

Suddenly it seemed to me that my wish was granted,
that my vision was rendered more acute, and I had the
faculty of discerning men's thoughts.   I congratulated
myself on having received this valuable gift, and pro-
ceeded to try its power.

Slowly I paced up and down the thoroughfare, reading at a glance the motives and purposes, the passions and affections, of each passer-by. I noticed two men at a street corner, conversing earnestly. The outward appearance of one was prepossessing in the highest degree. The other was a common-looking man of rustic garb and manner, but possessed of a goodly share of the yellow god. It was a lawyer whom he was consulting, and that gentleman was carefully and cautiously measuring the depth of his client's pocket. As they separated, I read beneath the lawyer's fine exterior these evil thoughts: "Ere this day twelve months, Brother Jonathan, with the help of luck and the devil, your heavy dollars will change owners."

"Alas for *justice!*" said I, and, with feelings somewhat dampened at this view of human nature, I passed along, and stepped into a dry goods store, where I had another opportunity for exercising my new power, by observing a persistent clerk put forth the superior quality of his goods in most eloquent terms to a lady customer, now and then paying a tribute to her vanity, by telling her that, "to be sure, it would not do for every lady to wear that style of goods; but really, such a fine figure would be set off to such advantage in those broad stripes and rich colors." This dose of flattery was quite irresistible, and decided the lady to take it; while the smart clerk gave himself a vast deal of credit for his success, saying boastingly to his fellow-clerk: "I made that dumpy creature really believe she had a pretty form. That's the way to get the extra shillings — just give their vanity a little stimulus; takes me to read human nature."

I wandered into the street again, and met an old man, the secret pages of whose life made me shudder at the atrocious crimes recorded there. Yet I knew him to be universally respected and revered for his wisdom and age. "Short-sighted humanity!" I sighed, and turned to read the next one. It was a woman, whose outward appearance was simply like other women, but in her heart I found a darker tragedy than was ever written out by pen.

The next was a doctor, and a genuine sinner. Thus ran his thoughts: "Now, if the poor fool had let me alone, he would have been well by this; but it's my good luck. Let's see: he is an influential man; I had better bring him as low as possible; make 'em think it 's a gone case, and then miraculously restore him. That will raise my reputation a peg or two; and then he has a deep pocket besides, which I shall have the pleasure of lightening." "Poor wretch," thought I, "how many human sacrifices you must answer for!"

Many time-worn friends I met, in whose hearts I found somewhat of envy, or jealousy, or malice, and my soul sickened at the sight, and I said bitterly: "My faith in them was little enough before, but it will be less hereafter."

Hitherto I had not found my new sense so much a source of pleasure as I had expected, but I would give it another trial; so I wandered into a church, and found myself just in time for the text, which was announced by the *holy* (?) man in this wise: "First Corinthians, tenth chapter, thirty-third verse. Even as I please all men in all things, *not seeking mine own profit,* but the profit of many, that they may be saved." By my increased powers of vision, I saw that his thoughts ran thus: "Now do your best to-day, and till you get the five hundred added to your salary, and then it will do to relax a little. That last sermon made a decided impression; you have only to confirm it by a few more such, to carry the point; then you may revel in two thousand a year." Feeling that I could not appreciate the sermon after this revelation, I left the house, now fully disgusted with the result of the new sense I had so eagerly desired.

"Enough, enough," I cried; "humanity is bad enough as we see it; let me look no more on such repulsive pictures! Would that the evil genius that conferred this gift, would take away the source of so much misery!" Suddenly, by the aid of a smart rap on my shoulder, I woke, to find myself in possession of five senses only, and have ever since thought them quite sufficient.

1858.

A Street Incident.

IT was as bright and keen a night
  As Christmas-time could show ;
The city thoroughfare was white
  With freshly fallen snow ;
The proud moon, from her sapphire throne,
  And myriad stars on high,
In cold and regnant splendor shone
  Down on the passers-by.

A human tide surged to and fro
  Along the busy mart,
Like a life-current's ebb and flow
  Through some gigantic heart :—
When little Archie, waiting, stayed
  Outside a fancy store,
Till grown-up sister Bertha said
  Her purchases were o'er :

Then took his tiny, mittened palm,
  And asked if he were tired.

"O, no! two fellows came along
　And halted, and inquired :
' Bub, what 's going on in Music Hall ?
　We 're strangers here, and Sonny,
Just tell us where to find some fun,
　And here 's some candy money ! '

"I did n't take it, Bertha, but
　I said, I 'll run and see ;
The Opera House was awful dark,
　And still as it could be !
I hurried back and told them so :
　They thanked me with a smile.
' Now Bill,' said one, where *shall* we go
　To kill time for a while ? '

" ' I do n't know, sirs,' I said, ' unless —
　There 's prayer-meeting close by.'
And then one looked so queer, I guess
　He 'd half a mind to cry !
The other said : ' By jingo, Bill,
　Let 's go ! ' and left me then.
They did n't, I am thinking still,
　Look much like meeting-men."

Happy-go-lucky, careless chaps
　Off on a " jolly lark,"
Made thoughtful for a space, perhaps.

By the child's naïve remark.
Who knows but in some world of light,
  In great books registered,
Are solemn vows, inspired that night
  By Archie's simple word!

To Miss Nellie N——.

——◆ ● ● ——

"HEART-WHOLE," you say you are, my friend,
    But really I must doubt it.
What!   Such an arrant flirt as you?
    The idea! why, I scout it!

O Nell, you know you can 't deny
    But once you had a passion
For poor St. John; you know 't was when
    Mustaches were the fashion.

That student, too, who studied more
    His fair inamorata
Than all the storied lore of his
    Neglected Alma Mater.

And then the way you served poor Hall,
    You surely can 't forget it,
And I shall not be much surprised
    If sometime you regret it.

There was a poet, too, you know,
    With whom you sometimes flirted.
Let 's see, who next ?   O, 't was for Brown
    The poet you deserted.

And he, I doubt not, soon will find
    That once a girl had tricked him,
While you, you coquette, glance around
    To find another victim.

" Heart-whole," indeed !   Why, it must be
    Divided 'mong so many,
That I am sometimes half in doubt
    If ever you had any !

Billy and I.

O! MANY a romping frolic,
  Have we had in the days gone by,
Through meadow and field and woodland —
  My beautiful Billy and I.
How fleetly he leaped the fences!
  How carefully over the stream
He carried his little mistress,
  Who was fearless as he, I ween!

Then I gathered the wildwood flowers
  His proud little head to deck,
Or wove them into a chaplet
  To hang round his arching neck.
Ah me! in the days of childhood,
  What very good friends were we!
For I own that I loved little Billy,
  And Billy, I'm sure, loved me.

He would lay his head on my shoulder
  In a gentle, caressing way,

Using such wiles to coax me
　　Again to the fields to play.
O! many a trick I 've served him.
　　And many has he served me :
For a more mischievous Billy
　　One never would wish to see.

Once in the spirit of mischief,
　　To see if he had any fears
Of his wild, tyrannical mistress,
　　I ventured to box his ears.
He waited until I mounted,
　　Then gave me a roguish look,
And then with a bound he threw me
　　Plump into the shallow brook.

O! many a romping frolic
　　We 've had in the days gone by,
Through meadow and field and woodland —
　　My dear little pony and I.
Ah, well-a-day! Time has changed us,
　　Since the days when together we played,
For Billy is now *an old farm horse.*
　　And I am old and staid.

The Teacher's Soliloquy.

(With Variations.)

O, WHAT high pride and pleasure I shall find
In watching here development of mind!
How grand the task to lead these tender youth
In paths of wisdom and in ways of truth!
My soul expands; the whole I contemplate;
To what great destiny, what noble fate,
I may direct, I would these little lives—
"Teacher, Ben Norton 's ben a swoppin' knives."

Some little pecadilloes I shall see,—
"O! Jennie Knight 's a stickin' pins in me!"
But I 'll not check their sweet, impulsive ways
Too rudely—rather will I seek to praise
When praise I can—and blame where blame is due—
"Teacher, Nell Burt 's a makin' mouths at you!"
The saucy midget! But they like their fun;
Still they must be demure now school 's begun.

Incipient poet, orator and sage
May be 'neath my assiduous tutelage—

Embryo presidents, perhaps, are here—
"O, teacher, Eddie Griffen boxed my ear!"
"Study your book, my love."   "Lesson ain't in it."
"Please, marm, may I go aout abaout a minute?"
I must be patient!   Rule my own soul well;
Thus shall an influence on their young hearts tell.

Wisely and lovingly I'll guide their feet
To learning's fount, to Helicon's water sweet—
"O, Carrie Merrill's eatin' sugar plumbs!"
"Ain't neither! only juthst I thucked my thumbs!"
The little elf!   My poor brain fairly whirls—
"Dan Rice is throwin' kisses to the girls!"
"That leetle feller hit me with his fist!"
O, what a crazy bedlam!   School's dismissed!

Little Irish Katie.

— ...

A CHILD came in at the open door,
And bashfully stood on the school-room floor;
Tattered, and barefoot, and freckled, and tanned,
A worn old book in her dimpled hand.
But *I* saw nothing as she stood there,
Only her marvelous, beautiful hair.

It seemed like a misplaced glory, lent
Perhaps from the head of her patron saint,
Red as a flame, and bright as gold,
Over her shoulders bare it rolled
In ripple, and curl, and sunbright wave
With the auburn warmth o'er which artists rave.

Sunburnt and plain was the Irish child,
Her form uncouth and her manners wild,
Rude, and neglected, and poor, and mean,
Was all of life *she* had ever seen,
But a princess royal might have prayed
For the crown of that little Irish maid.

She sat just there, by the school-room wall,
There where the softest light doth fall
Down through the elm tree's trailing tress,—
The ragged lassie would little guess
I put her there for the strong effect
Of sun and shadow, all mottled and flecked.

All changing and wonderful, with its beams
Losing themselves amid warmer gleams
Of the tangled, auburn mass of hair,
That fell like a halo around her there,—
Yes—there she sat, with a studious look,
Poring over her spelling-book.

One day I missed her ;—the small, bright head
With its wealth of curls, on a poor child's bed
Was tossing and moving in wild unrest:
And then a Presence—a phantom guest
Came in at the door—and then they said
Little Irish Katie, alas ! was dead.

8

Annie.

...

WHEN the roses bloom again,
  One will stand here by my side,
I shall bear another name,
  I shall be a happy bride.
He will haste from lands afar,
  Soon as roses are abloom,
From the fearful sounds of war,
  Shrieking shell, and cannon boom.

He will come with glory crowned,
  And to me the brave deeds tell.
Often in the gloaming hour,
  When together we shall dwell.
Ah, dear Lord: Thou deign'st to fill
  My life chalice to the brim:
One request I crave Thee still:
  Oh, let me be worthy him!

When the roses bloom again; —
  Thus she thought but did not speak,

And the bright blood sent its flame
    Upward into either cheek —
While upon her bridal robe
    Deftly those young fingers wrought ;
Wove she, in its broiderie,
    Many a prayer and thought.

O, the noble life, and high,
    That went out that self-same night,
Underneath the Southern sky,
    On a bloody field of flight !
Still she sang, in cadence sweet,
    Sweet and low down in her heart :
Soon my Hero I shall meet,
    Never, never more to part !

When the rose blooms came again,
    Ere their earliest scent had died,
Ah ! she bore another name,
    Ah ! she was a fair, fair bride.
Still and cold, yet fair and sweet,
    Not in dainty, wedding dress,
But in ghastly winding sheet,
    Lay she in her loveliness.

Beautiful upon her bier,
    With the pale buds in her hair,

Annie! we had called her here,
  Angel! they would know her there.

Maidens twelve, in solemn train,
  Bearing rose blooms white and red,
Chanted low a sad refrain,
  As they circled round the dead.

          Miserere! Miserere!
Heaven is bright, if Earth is dreary —
  Take her now, oh Earth our Mother,
Thou wilt fold her as none other,
  Till the judgment, keep our trust,
This beloved, holy dust,
  Warden! unto whom is given
What unlocks the gate of Heaven,
  Open your celestial portal,
For the ransomed soul, immortal!
          Miserere! Miserere!
  Heaven is bright, though Earth be dreary.

A Temperance Tale.

As Told by my Grandfather.

• • • —

OLD Cooper King had a bright little son,
A mischievous juvenile brimming with fun ;
But one drop of bitterness poisoned his joy
When he thought of himself as a poor drunkard's
    boy.

Oft he was sent to the small village store,
Thro' woods dark and lonely, a mile or more,
With a jug half hidden, ingeniously,
And his own sad musings for company.

Bluebird, and robin, and bobolink gay,
Swallow and thrush, at each break of day,
Filled all the welkin with pæans sweet
As ever a mortal ear did greet.

They sang so madly above his head,
That he fell to interpreting what they said,
And thought their melody mocking him,
As he trod the path thro' the forest dim.

One bright June morn the empty old jug
Was hidden again 'neath the elbow snug;
But the nimble feet were tardy and slow,
Till his father thundered, "Why do n't you go?"

"Cos," whimpered the child, as he trembling stood,
"Please, sir, I'm afraid to go through the wood."
"What now?" yelled King, with a drunken leer.
"Cos somethin' talks to me awful queer.

"It says," (and he keyed his voice up high,
And looked in his father's bloodshot eye,)
'Where you going? where you going?'
'Down t' the store! down t' the store!'
'What after? what after?'
'Bottle o' rum! bottle o' rum!'
'Who's it for? who's it for?'
'Cooper King! Cooper King!'
'Drink it up! Drink it up!'
'Send again! Send again!'
'Che-arge it! Che-arge it!'"

'T was the little brown thrasher, a comical rogue,
Whose song the boy chattered in dialogue;
And such was the mortified man's chagrin,
'T is said he forever quit drinking gin.

A Memory.

...

To-day I heard an organ's tone,
   Tender and tremulous and low,
Making a scarce articulate moan,
   So soft and sweet, so sad and slow.

Then wild and passionate it flowed,
   As if behind its brazen breast
A heart all human burned and glowed
   With strange and feverish unrest.

Anon a pleading, piteous cry,
   And then a grand triumphal strain,
Then sinks to a delicious sigh
   That faints and breathes and faints again.

The many-throated organ spoke
   Of what naught else can speak to me:
Its mellow cadences awoke
   A buried precious memory.

Spoke of an old church, vast and dim :
   Spoke of a golden sunset hour ; —
I heard not priest, but only him
   Who swept those chords with wondrous power.

Through stainéd glass the sunset clouds
   A tide of gorgeous glory rolled.
Altar and shrine were wrapt in shrouds
   Of amber, amethyst and gold.

Silent and thrilled with rapturous awe,
   I sat in love's sweet mystery —
For eye has answered eye — I saw
   Those chords were struck for me.

They spoke to me through that wild strain,
   They poured out all my heart's desire :
Spoke till joy grew exquisite pain,
   Spoke from a mad youth's heart of fire.

The Voluntary died away,
   Tender and sweet it died at last.
The sunset clouds had turned to gray,
   When from the dim old church we passed.

Thou Art My God.

— •••

Oh God, thou art my God; thou art thy own blessedness, the center of thy own desires, and the boundless spring of thy own happiness. Thou art immutable and infinitely perfect, and therein consists thy blessedness and glory; but thou art my God; it is from thence flows all my consolation; this glorious privilege is my dignity and boast. Thou art my God, and I will praise thee. I love thee, and I will exalt thee. I have all things, in possessing thee; I find no want, no void within; my wishes are answered, and all my desires appeased, when I believe my title to thy favor secure.

Whatever tempests arise, whatever darkness surrounds me, yet thou art my God. I cry to thee, and the storms cease, and the darkness vanishes.

I find my expectations from the World disappointed, friends false, and human dependence vain; but still thou art my God, my unfailing confidence, my rock, my everlasting inheritance. Death and the Enemy hurl their darts against me; but, with a fearless and tranquil heart,

I cry, Thou art my God; I dwell on high; my place of defense is the munitions of rocks.

While thou art mine, what can I fear? Can Omnipotence be vanquished? can almighty strength be opposed? When it can, then, and not till then, shall I want security; then, and not till then, shall my confidence be shaken and my hopes confounded. Thou art my God; let me again repeat the glorious accents, and hear the pleasurable sounds; let me a thousand and a thousand times repeat it; it is rapture all, and harmony. The harps of angels and their tongues, what notes more melodious could they sing or play, what but these transporting words give the emphasis to all their joys? On this they dwell; it is their eternal theme.

Thou art my God. Like me every seraph boasts the glorious property, and owes his happiness to those important words; in them unbounded joys are comprehended. Paradise itself, all heaven, is here described; all that is possible to be uttered of celestial blessedness is here contained.

My God, my triumph and my glory, let others boast of what they will, and pride themselves in human securities; let them place their confidence in their wealth, their honor, and their numerous friends; I renounce all earthly dependence, and glory only in my God.

When death shall remove all other supports, and force me to quit my title to the dearest names below, in my God I shall have an unchangeable property; that engagement shall remain firm, when I shall loose my hold of other engagements. Then, all human things will vanish with an everlasting flight; I shall bid them a joyful adieu, and breathe out my soul with this triumphant exclamation: Thou art my God, my eternal possession! Nor death, nor any thing, shall ever separate me from thy love.

Thou art my God. Let me survey the extent of my blessedness; let me take a prospect of my vast possession; let me consider its dimensions. Oh height! oh depth! oh length! and breadth immeasurable! I have all that is worth possessing. Thou art my God. But what have I uttered? Is mortality permitted to speak these daring words? Can any of the human race make such glorious pretensions? Thou thyself canst give no more,—thou that art thy own happiness, and the spring of joy to all thy creatures; with thee are the fountains of pleasure, and in thy presence is fullness of joy. Immortal life and happiness flow from thee; and they are necessarily blessed who are surrounded with thy favor. Thou art their God, and thou art my God to everlasting.

Sunday Morning.

...

O, BLESSINGS on the water-cure!
Refreshing, cool, abundant, pure;
That cleanses from the grime, and soil,
And clinging trace of week-day toil:
I revel in the healthful flood,
And think meanwhile of Jesus' blood
For mortal stains; O, in His sight,
To-day may I be clean and white.

Before the looking-glass I stand,
And brush long tresses through my hand:
The mirror, with no flaw nor crack,
A faithful copy answers back;
O, that I might, without defect,
My Saviour's image thus reflect;
Not with distorted, fitful show,
But true enough for all to know.

Comely and clean, externally,
I 've often, always longed to be;

But do I care to be, meanwhile,
Inwardly fair and free from guile?
But yesterday I saw some lace
I wanted more than Christian grace!
Or some insignia of wealth,
Desired far more than moral health!

I think the enemy comes to us,
Sometimes with childish trifles thus:
And we, off guard, and unawares,
Fall into such transparent snares.
O, shame! Sad, sorry shame, that I
Should e'er forget my calling high!
Forgive, forget, O Saviour dear,
The pitfalls that I come so near!

Now be the garments fresh and clean,
Seemly and plain, to worship in!
It does not matter what the dress,
So I have Jesus' righteousness:
And though some curious eyes might stare,
I'm glad there's One who does n't care,
Who knoweth life consisteth not
In what we have, or have n't, got.

Of perishing and worldly store,
Help me to covet nothing more
Than Thy far-reaching scrutiny,

Dear Master, seeth best for me.
The bells are ringing, sweet and wild,
Heaven's call to many a homesick child:
Hither to church we fondly come:
'T is Father's house — and therefore home.

Now give the "hearing ear," I pray,
For what the good man has to say;
Give the appreciative mind,
Swift to discern, and sure to find
Kernels of truth, and seeds of good
Presented for the spirit's food;
And may this Sabbath morn draw me
Solemnly, sweetly, nearer Thee.

Willie on the Shining Shore.

O, MAMMA, darling mamma, I have reached the
  Better Land —
Just as I seemed to sink away, and slip from your
  fond hand,
Just as my little feet had touched the cold, cold
  wave of death,
And when, with one poor broken gasp, I yielded up
  my breath,
The gentle Shepherd met me, and He took me
  safely o'er;
Close sheltered in His bosom, I gained the Shining
  Shore;
And through all the Valley's shadows, and the
  River's dreaded flow,
I had no thought of danger, for I trusted Jesus so.

And, mamma, could you see me now, with Faith's
  untroubled eye,

You would check your bitter grieving, you would
hush the choking sigh,
And with more than mortal radiance your tearful
face would shine,
Could you look on Heaven's glories, and know its
bliss is mine.
I know you miss me in the home you builded there
below,
And Willie's room is but a place for anguished tears
to flow;
Your house is empty of its joy, your heart is very
sore,
For you miss dear little Willie so, but Heaven would
miss him more.

And I can not fold my glistening wings and hush the
golden lyre,
That I have learned to strike so rapturously, with
all the angel choir,
I can not leave my victor's crown, my robes of
shining white,
Touched in every fold with glory such as ne'er
blessed mortal sight.
For my ransomed spirit would not dare to risk its
chance again,
'Mid Earth's manifold temptations, its trials, and
its pain;

But I 'm safe beyond all sorrow, and sin, and sick-
    ness here,
And my feet can never go astray, in Heaven, mamma,
    dear.

So you will not grieve too sorely, with great sobs
    and anguish wild.
Mamma, Papa, you are coming some day hither, to
    your child —
And the years will not be joyless, nor too long and
    lone your stay.
If you still can trust the Master, with submissive
    hearts alway;
Then, when all the journey 's ended, and you reach
    the pearly gate,
Just within the glowing portal, Mamma, Papa, I
    shall wait;
And while all the angel legions smite their sweet,
    sweet, harps anew,
I, your little angel Willie, will be first to welcome
    you.

9

On Receiving an Anonymous Gift.

My bonnie big box, my box of blue,
Pray, where did you come from, what are you?
An irreverent school-boy's joke, mayhap,
Venting his genius in trick or trap.
Up with the cover, off with the lid,
I 'll see what secret is 'neath it hid!
What mischievous scheme is here I 'll know!
If any young rebel dares to—— Oh!
What intoxicating perfume is this?
Like the breath of a goddess, a fairy's kiss;
Like airs from vintage hills afar,
Methinks these spicy breathings are;
They might have floated from Italy's shore,
Or from grapes of Eshcol in Scripture lore;
And something more than imprisoned wine
Lurks in these bounties of the vine,
Uprising now with the fruity smell,
A subtle something that blendeth well,
A blessed and charming attribute,
Not always found with pleasant fruit;

This doth my heart a captive lead,
The fragrance of a loving deed.
Each tiny globe, and each purple sphere,
Nestled in tempting clusters here,
Enfoldeth something sweeter far
Than even its own rich juices are :
Something in ambush I can see,
A thought — a friend's dear thought for me ;
Outweighing pearls from ocean grot,
That friendly, beautiful, kindly thought.
Here's white and purple and red and blue,
With every shade and in every hue :
Cheek against cheek in their ripened bloom,
Drunk in their own exquisite perfume ;
Here's " Agawam," " Wilder," and " Delaware,"
Tucked in with graceful skill and care,
With " Merrimac," " Concord," " Allen's," " Iona,"
But never a hint of the cunning donor :
But I can guess whose generous hand
And heart, my bonnie blue box, have planned,
Whose dainty fingers and artist eye,
Grouped cluster on cluster lavishly ;
" Not letting even the left hand know,"
Because the Master hath taught her so,
In her gracious and loving ministry,
Nameless and silent, as sphinx could be.
Ah, bonnie blue box, and treasures bright,
You 're filling my mouth, and my heart, to-night.

On Watch Hill.

— •••

I sit and watch the ships go by,
  Gliding so softly o'er the sea,
I hear the breakers swelling high
  A moaning all so drearily —

And all my soul is filled with pain:
  For I recall my vanished youth,
When *my* ship sailed upon the main
  Freighted with love and trust and truth.

Proudly she sat upon life's wave,
  A goodly ship and fair to see.
Years passed, long years, and nothing save
  A broken wreck returned to me.

O bitterness and grief untold!
  I drag out still a life of woe,
E'er since the angry waters rolled
  Above my hopes of long ago.

Vainly I cry to Earth and Heaven,
   Vainly I fly from East to West :
To my sad soul no peace is given,
   For me the wild Earth holds no rest.

And thus beside the Sea, alone,
   I sit through long hours silently,
In harmony with ocean's moan
   Telling her mournful tales to me.

Far on the blue horizon line
   A white sail toward me seems to float.
Some heart it thrills—but, oh ! not mine—
   Some fond eyes watch that distant boat —

Some lips grow prayerful as she sails,
   Perhaps before unused to pray,
And plead Heaven's gentlest, kindest gales
   To follow on her shining way.

But on the white beach just below,
   A ruined, stranded vessel lies :
Toward her my sympathies shall flow,
   For her the tears swell in my eyes.

Her usefulness and beauty o'er,
   Despoiled of all her grace and pride,

She'll triumph on the wave no more.
   No more the restless waters ride.

The sea gulls spread their snowy wings.
   And ships go on to ports unknown:
The summer zephyr weirdly sings,
   My sad thoughts chant an undertone.

I look afar, with hopeless eye,
   Across the boundless, heaving sea:
No ship of mine can I descry,
   No loving soul looks out for me.

O sea, moan on, forever moan,
   And tell your sorrows o'er and o'er!
Methinks your grief is like mine own.
   To be forgotten never more.

Thanksgiving Memories.

...

I GLANCE around the festal board,
    But one is missing there—
We need not wait—there still will be
    One little, empty chair.

Twelve months ago this very time,
    We laid our pet away.
O never can my heart forget
    That sad Thanksgiving day.

And then the " Merry Christmas" came,
    And then the gay New Year's;
But unto us the holidays
    Brought naught but grief and tears.

What had we then for which to lift
    Our hearts in thankfulness?
What was there left in earth and heaven
    For which our God to bless?

Was he a God of love who thus
    Could take our only one ?
To thus deserve such chastisement,
    What great sin had we done ?

Hush, murmuring heart, and learn to say :
    " E'en tho' Thou slayest me,
And tho' our sorrows multiply,
    Yet will we trust in Thee."

Dear little boy ! a year in Heaven !
    Why, then, should we repine ?
'T is better thus—and yet I would
    Thy sinless death were mine.

I would that in thy quiet grave
    This weary heart might lie ;
But patience, heart ! and bide thy time.
    Thou 'lt rest there, by-and-by.

                     November, 1859.

Christmas Carol.

FOR A CHILD.

— • •

Far away to the eastward,
  In the beautiful Orient land,
The land that is rich in tradition
  And legends, so old and so grand,—
Far back in the long past ages,
  One luminous, starry morn,
In this land of historic glory,
  The Prince I serve was born.

Not in a lordly castle —
  Not in a palace fine —
Not in a home ancestral,
  Was born this Prince of mine ; —
Not on a monarch's pillow
  They laid his royal head ;
Not on a couch of costly down —
  But — in a manger — bed.

And kingly robes He wore not,
    Nor ever a jeweled crown ;
Nor bore He scepter or signet,
    This Prince of strange renown.
Yet kingdoms, strong and ancient,
    And the whole Earth's throned powers,
Shook, to their mighty centers,
    For this mightier Prince of ours.

So, ever through all the ages,
    We celebrate His birth,
Who, though he slept in a manger,
    Was Lord of all heaven and earth.
And ever under His banner
    We 'll fight against every sin,
Till into our dear Lord's kingdom
    He gathers His children in.

Thoughts on Watch Night.

Written between 10 and 12 o'clock on the
31st of December, 1860.

• • •

HARK, the death-knell now is ringing
　Of the old year.　I would heed it
E'er the new one comes in, bringing
　Its new duties.　I would profit
By remembering all the blessings
　With which God has strewn my way,—
How he's watched me, without ceasing,
　Kept from danger, night and day.

I 'd remember, death's dark angel
　Has not entered my loved home :
God has spared my dear ones still ;
　I 'm not left in grief alone.
I remember now, with sorrow,
　Other days and other years
When no light dawned on the morrow,
　But my heart was filled with fears.

Life's charm was broken; in the grave
  Was buried all my earthly hopes.
God's word alone had power to save;
  His arm could bear the mourner up.
O, I thank thee, blessed Saviour,
  For thy promises of love
To the weary, heavy laden;
  There is rest for them above.

I have often sinned against thee,
  Often grieved thy Holy Spirit.
Now, I beg thee, O forgive me,
  Through my Saviour's dying merit,
Grant me grace to live more holy,
  Grace to keep these solemn vows:
More like Jesus, meek and lowly,
  Humbly to God's will I'd bow.

— ⸱→⸱

These lines were written between 12 and
2 o'clock, January 1st, 1861.

Now, the new year, I have entered,
  The past has gone, with joys and cares.
Borne to Heaven its truthful record,
  My many sins are written there;

But all across the long, dark list
    Now is written—" All forgiven."
Now feels my heart this consciousness,
    And with joy can think of Heaven.

With faith in God and the golden rule
    To guide my steps, with a loving heart
And cheerful face, through life's rough school
    Kind words to all, bear well my part
In life's great contest : forgetting never
    Those who 've crossed death's chilly river,—
Not parted forever, gone only before,
    Await my coming, on the other shore.

Introductory for Santa Claus.

FOR A LITTLE BOY.

• • • —

Last night the fairies came to me, and told a wondrous tale
Of a queer and quaint old fellow, all clad in frozen
mail:
With beautiful and varied gifts his back was laden
high;
And they said we all should know him by the
twinkle in his eye.

Then their small bells seemed to tinkle, and the
fairies danced away,
While I dreamily lay, thinking of that *first* Christmas day,
When some shepherds on the mountains, in the
morning star-light clear,
Went to find *their* gift from Heaven—the Christ-
babe of Judea.

O. how sweet to think of Jesus! when we 're all so
    happy made
By the Christmas gifts and greetings!
But I see you are afraid
I shall spin too long a story. So here I 'll make a
    pause,
To introduce our jolly friend, the brave old Santa
    Claus.

1865.

Charles Howard Warriner.

Drowned July 8, 1866, aged 11 years.

———•••———

Rest! rest! young brother.
  Sweetly, safely rest!
Not in arms of Mother,
  Not on Father's breast!
Not where dream or vision
  Shall thy sleep annoy;
But in fields Elysian,
  Rest! our darling boy!

Death's cruel river,
  With its ice-cold wave,
Made thy young heart shiver,
  In its watery grave.
But Jesus met thee
  On the brighter shore,
Then why regret thee,
  Blest forever more!

Peace! peace! bereaved ones.
    'T was the Father's will:
For all Earth's grieved ones
    He has comfort still.
When God shall need you,
    Charlie's little hand
May be the first to lead you
    To the angel band.

10

To My Friend Across the Way,

— ••• —

'T is a fair and childish brow,
Wreathed with bridal flowers now,
And a serious, timid grace
Seems to gather on her face ;
For the solemn words are spoken,
Never, trust we, to be broken !

Blessings on thee, bonny bride !
Prayers and blessings multiplied !
Sacred promise, holy vow,
Each to each, ye 've given now,
Vowed to honor, love, and cherish —
Till this changeful life shall perish.

Trusting, loyal little wife !
Farewell now the girlish life,
Farewell now its childish joys,
All that maiden thoughts employs.

With another's fate is blended
Thine, henceforth, till fate is ended.

No foreboding doubts or fears.
Clouds for the blithe New Year —
Be it fraught with weal or woe.
Smiles or tears, we may not know,
Yet we tenderly confide thee,
To the strong, fond heart beside thee.

May this tender, new relation
Make all happy compensation
For the loss of Father, Mother,
Gentle Sister, loving Brother;
And the Husband be to you
Ever noble, good and true.

Heaven's eternal care be o'er thee!
Whatsoever be before thee!
Angels fold their wings above thee,
And the good Lord ever love thee!
And a happy, useful life.
Crown the bride, a *perfect* wife!

Lines

TO

MR. AND MRS. CHARLES C. BARRETT,

On the death of their little girl, who died at South Hadley
Falls, February 25th, 1868, aged three years.

— ••• —

LITTLE GERTIE,
Baby, sleep! And softyly rest
On His gentle, loving breast,
Who the little children bless.

Fold your dainty, waxen palms!
Mother's fond, encircling arms ˙
Could not save from all earth's harms!

Sweet as sweetest flowers that blow!
Pure as˙Heaven's whitest snow!
And they loved you, loved you so!

Every winning, childish grace,
In your little cold, still face,
Now with broken hearts they trace.

With a mother's doting care,
Curl once more the soft, bright hair
Round the childish brow so fair.

To their long and calm repose,
Those sweet eyes, oh! softly close —
And your life — how dark it grows!

All the toys she used in play
Lay in blinding tears away —
Ah! that *she* should know decay!

Ah! that she, the darling one,
Must be hidden from the sun
Underneath the church-yard stone!

Is she there? No: never more
Think it, mother, grieved and sore, —
She's "not lost, but gone before."

Baby sleeps! but is not dead!
Mother-heart, be comforted:
Cease regretful tears to shed.

After days of toil and pain,
You with ransomed ones may reign,
And may have your child again!

The Silver Wedding.

(S. L. P.)

——— • • • —

LOOKING backward down the dim aisles of the
    shadowy vanished years,
Many a picture, fair and lovely, oft before my mind
    appears ;
And the vision that comes floating back to Memory
    to-night,
Had I but a limner's pencil, I would sketch in colors
    bright : —

Where, in mansions quaint and olden, lights are
    flashing to and fro ;
Figures robed in festive raiment o'er the threshold
    come and go ;
All the chivalry and beauty of the fine old country
    place,
With their youth and joy and laughter, meet a
    wedding scene to grace.

Soon a white gleam and a rustle—then, on all as
    silence falls,
Bride and bridegroom now are coming down the
    wide, old-fashioned hall,
And unshadowed brows grow earnest while a few
    low words are said,
Then a prayer and benediction, and the twain one
    flesh are wed.

Years glide on, and children gather in the new and
    pleasant home.
Scarce a shadow on the hearthstone of their dwell-
    ing dares to come.
Calm and placid flows their life-stream, blessed in
    basket and in store.
No death summons breaks the circle from the dim
    and unknown shore.

Still the years glide ever onward till the Silver
    Wedding day
Dawns as blithely as the other in the Past so far
    away,
And the messages are scattered 'mong the old
    friends far and wide,
Bidding home full many a matron who went forth
    a bonny bride:

Bidding home full many a hero to Northampton's
    hills once more.

Where beneath its bold twin mountains he may call
     back days of yore,
And forget his care-seamed forehead and the dear
     wife's fading eye,
Dreaming they are boy and maiden as in years so
     long gone by.

Thus it was the white-winged missive bringing
     pleasantly to mind
Many a fond association of the days of " Auld Lang
     Syne "
Came to us—and we would gather fain with you,
     did time allow—
But accept our hearty greetings and the wishes
     offered now.

May your onward path be upward, and your lives
     with usefulness
Be so rich and full and fragrant, all the poor your
     names shall bless.
May your feet tread thornless roses down life's
     gradual decline,
And good deeds fill up the remnant of the days
     which still are thine.

When at last these glad occasions here for evermore
     shall cease,
Like a river's steady current be your soul's unruffled
     peace,

Nor your barks be long divided which so long have
    sailed life's sea.
When you launch out on the ocean that we call
    Eternity.

1869.

Farewell to the Old Church.

— ...

AND now farewell—a fond farewell, to this long hal-
    lowed place
Where oft the Lord hath deigned to bless His people
    with his grace :
Where many a weary, sin-sick soul and many a
    heavy heart
With Mary, loved of Jesus, hath chosen the better
    part.

And some, I know, who erst with us these sacred
    aisles have trod,
A sainted band, now worship in the City of our
    God,
In temples builded not with hands, eternal in the
    skies,
Where, by the healing stream of Life, celestial
    palms arise.

So as the old church crumbles and we gather here
    no more.

We 'll cherish blessed memories of loved ones gone
before :
We 'll gratefully remember how the Lord hath met
us here,
And trust his wonderous mercy for every future
year.

Now, in the holy Master's work, let every one
engage,
From fair-haired child and rosy youth to silver-
headed age :
And every face set Zionward, we 'll strive to follow
them
Who have gone to worship yonder in the New
Jerusalem.

November, 1869.

A Holiday.

— ••• —

BILLY is at the door. "All aboard!" And there's a hurried fastening of hats under back hair, a donning of gauntlets and dusters, and the "women folks," with Willie, the little guest, are off for a holiday.

"What shall we do with the house?" asks careful Marmee, who generally bides at home. "Why, we can't take it with us!" responds Lucy. "I'll look out for it." calls *pater familias* in a stentorian voice, making off in an opposite direction, and we are morally certain he will never think of it again until dinner time. So we prudently lock the doors, and with characteristic consistency leave every window open, but trust that closed blinds will have an inhospitable look to the traditional "tramp" and decide him to pass on. Spot wags his tail in anticipation. "No, no, Spottie, you must stay on guard!" And the wistful look changes to one of dejected obedience.

Ten minutes' ride, and we are in the land of "wooden nutmegs and cast-iron hams."

Billy ambles on, in ruminating mood, and, knowing well the indulgent charioteer, occasionally turns aside for a mouthful of leaves from a wayside bush, or a taste of juicy grass by the road. Past shaven fields we glide, and pleasant farmhouses where the matrons are out amid the bean-poles selecting "garden sass" for the noonday meal, or spreading their milk-pans to the sweetening sun ; through wide old country streets, with an air of prim respectability about the homes on either hand, and a hint of their owner's conservatism in the rigid rows of holly-hocks and sunflowers from door to gateway; anon through narrow lanes, fringed with uncut bushes, eye and ear are caught, here by a nimble chip-monk racing with us along the stone wall, and there by a meadow lark, as he sings with roguish cunning and sweet, inimitable inflec-tions, "I—see you! You can't—see—me!"

Just at the base of a bold mountain range our way has been, but now we turn sharply, and begin to ascend. Very slowly we climb, after the late exciting race with Bunnie. A precipice on our right hand, a slender railing dividing it from the road, and walls of forbidding ledges on the left. A little gloomy and weird, it seems, as if a highwayman's chosen spot, but lo! emerging from its umbrageous gloom, what a view is spread before us! We draw rein and stand erect. A happy valley, by frowning, wooded mountains guarded, and in its midst the north pond of the group known as Southwick Ponds lies dimp-ling in the sunshine. Gazing with many ejaculations of delight, we descry, at wide intervals, a section of a brown roof, a group of cattle grazing, the white stones of a little graveyard, and a distant spire lifting its slender finger above the foliage. But we never could stop long at such an altitude, and Billy is admonished to "go on."

Here is a noble homestead, and the white-headed octogenarian sits in the shade, a book upon his knee. "It's old Captain Pollns, I must speak to him," says Marmee, and we halt again. Many stories are told of this man's physical and spiritual prowess. A "powerful exhorter" in the days of early Methodism, his presence gave an inspiration to "the means o' grace," and character to the community. "I'm reading the book o' the Martyrs," says the old saint. "I've read it a many times: but I want to read it again." This man, in his prime, would have eclipsed modern gymnastic feats and "health-lifts" marvels. The boys of two generations later love still to tell how, when he was coming down an icy mountain with an ox-sled of wood, and something gave way threatening much damage, he loosed the "off" ox from the yoke, stepped into his place, and sustained his share of the load with the "nigh" one to the foot of the hill. They tell, too, of his lifting a baby colt each successive day from its birth till it was a full-grown horse.

Now we come to a country school-house. The little tow-heads, stealing furtive glances from the windows, are too great an attraction for one of our party, and by great grace and clemency she is allowed to stop and visit the institution.

"What shall we do, while we wait for her?"

" Do n't you want some water ? "

" I do," says Willie.

" We 'll make an errand in here for some."

How pleased about something the girl looks who comes
to the door, as does also the matron within. A few
greetings and out it comes : twins at this house, just a
week old ! " Do n't you want to see them ? " We tiptoe
into a great shady room, with a beautiful old-fashioned,
striped carpet possessing fifty years of history all its own,
and there 's the cradle ! We hold our breath ! The
father reaches out a great bronzed but loving hand to
lay off the netting, and we stare down upon a pair of
the daintiest, demi-semi-quavers of humanity you ever
saw. In comes nurse, a handsome woman of fifty, with
wavy gray hair.

" Is n't this Mrs. ——? "

" Yes."

" I thought so ; you do n't know me. Just look at me
a minute, though it 's twenty years since you 've seen me."
Marmee cudgels her brain, and ransacks the attic of her
memory, but has to do what Pompey did with the
conundrum, " gub 'er up." The lady jogs her treacher-
ous recollection, and then what a hand-shaking ! what
laughing ! and they launch out into a tide of retrospec-
tions. Apprehensive of delay, we wedge in a question :
" How far is it to Copper Hill?" " Two miles." And
we make our adieus and journey on.

A few minutes later, and we behold the object of

our excursion. This is Newgate—the old Connecticut State Prison, long since abandoned for the present institution at Wethersfield. The iron bars and massive walls, even in ruins, chill us with their threatening aspect. We tie our steed in the shade of a chestnut, and proceed to make the tour. Into the stone-paved court, past the tread-mill, up the dilapidated stairs of ancient workshops, down into subterranean bake-rooms, with mammoth boilers, and ovens, and cauldrons, we wander; up again to the ponderous stone-wall that was formerly ornamented on the top by quantities of rough, jagged pieces of glass cemented in edgewise, so that the convicts should cruelly cut their hands and be compelled to desist if they attempted to escape by scaling this wall.

Several parties are here to-day, picnicing under the trees across the way, or grouped with unconscious picturesqueness among the ruins. Here is a fine old country gentleman, who pays the chaperon very acceptably for a little time, and contributes many an anecdote for our delectation.

"I used to come here seventy years ago," he says, "on a Sunday, to see them prisoners come into chapel, by couples, their feet shackled, and an iron chain going between their legs the whole length of the gang."

"You must have been a little fellow," we insinuate.

"Yes, yes," he muses, "my father fetched the first prisoner that was ever brought here. He was a young chap: he'd stole twenty cents from a bar in Hartford, and they put him in here, down in the hole for twenty-four hours."

" Tell us all about the mines."

" Well, you see there 's copper here," picking up a specimen of the ore. " but it did n't never pay for working. Before the Revolutionary War they sent a whole ship-load on to England, to have it tested, and she wan't never heard from. Then, during the Revolution, they used to catch the Tories and put 'em down in the mine for safe-keeping, before this 'ere prison was built."

" Did prisoners ever escape ?"

" Well, not easy. You see there 's a dry well down below, where they used to draw up the ore in buckets worked by horse-power. Well, they said that old Captain Viets' daughter, that lived in that big house you see across the road ('t was a tavern then), fell in love with one of the prisoners and helped him to escape up that dry well. Then some of 'em did try to mine out 'way through the mountain. They was all put down in the hole to sleep always, and I expect some o' the desprit ones used to spend a good part o' the nights borin'. Leastwise the keepers discovered they 'd tunneled a right smart distance."

" Did you ever hear me tell Abbe's story, girls ?" says Marmee.

" Yes, ages ago, but tell it again."

" Your grandmother and I were paring apples late one night. I was about sixteen. The boys, your Uncles

11

Thad and Lucius and Henry, had been off to general training that day, and had come home tired, and hung their coats up in the old kitchen. Your Aunt Delia had finished a fine shirt for one of them, and hung that upon a peg. Every body was abed but we two. All at once we heard a noise. It was about half past eleven. We listened, and soon it was repeated—a little clank. 'Something's wrong at the barn,' says your grandmother. 'May be some of the cattle have got loose. We won't call your father; you get the lantern, and we'll go out and see.' So I lit the lantern. We went out to the barn, and found every thing all right and safe; then we went in, put things to rights, and went to bed."

"Next morning the new fine shirt, one of the boys' coats, and two or three other things, were gone. We never locked a door in those days, and two days after, we heard that a convict had escaped from Newgate. Still, as we lived a dozen miles away, we hardly connected the two events; but months after, when snow came, and they were getting out the old sleigh for use, they chanced to open the box and found in it a whole suit of convict's clothes, half gray and half black, you know, together with the shackles. It was his struggling to get rid of these we heard that night, though a marvel how he ever succeeded. Well, brother Thad put them up and brought them over here to Newgate, and undid them before the warden, who exclaimed, 'You've got Abbe!' 'No.' 'But these are what he wore away,' said the warden. And. girls, Abbe never was caught nor heard from to this day."

A family lives in the old warden's house. We interview the matron.

" Can we go down into the mines ? "

" Yes, but your gowns won't be white when you come up. You can 't go without candles. I keep 'em to sell for ten cents apiece. There ain't no man to go down with ye."

Gowns are a secondary consideration, but her last suggestion becomes an imperative necessity the more we think of it.

" I won't go down with you alone." says Lucy mysteriously. and refuses to demonstrate the " why." We whip off the daisy heads with our parasols and consider. Meanwhile Marmee has slipped off to a couple of gentlemen that have just appeared on the scene. How she contrived to flatter them into compliance we shall never know, but the exigencies of the hour developed her talents as the " maneuvering mamma " to a degree before undreamed of. and. presto ! the aforesaid gentlemen were at our service.

We go around the warden's house, down a slight declivity. and open a door into a little brick dungeon.

We see an open trap a yard square, and a stout ladder leading perpendicularly into the vault. The ladder is fastened with iron bands into the solid rock. One after another we peer into the gloom and retreat appalled.

"Any ghosts down there?" laughs the younger of our "impressed" gallants; and after little badinage as to who shall pioneer, we make the descent, holding the flaring candle aloft with one desperate grip, and the ladder rounds with the other. The day is intensely hot, but a clammy chill pervades the cavern. Our hero above mentioned begins to spout Shakespeare with tragic tones and gestures: "I am thy father's spirit." etc., "doing" the ghost scene in Hamlet. We clap our hands and cry "bravo!" and telegraph to Lucy, "college boy." Little Willie gets a more tenacious hold of Lucy's hand. Sometimes we walk erect, bumping our heads now and then, and sometimes the rocky roof compels us to play the quadruped while we grope through winding passages with spinal columns accommodated to the situation. The gentlemen are devoted. A ready hand is constantly extended to aid our uncertain movements, the sedate elder remarking, in a tone of mock comfort, "the pink roses on your hat are spoiled;" and the younger, in sepulchral chest tones, beginning to a

> "Tale unfold, whose lightest word
> Would harrow up the soul; freeze thy young blood;
> Make thy two eyes, like stars, start from their spheres;
> Thy knotted and combined locks to part,
> And each particular hair to stand on end,
> Like quills upon the fretful porcupine."

Willie, little man, has been brave till now, but this is the drop too much. He implores us to ascend. "Soon, dear."

Ha, yonder is a gleam of light! We hasten forward. A little pond, and a light reflected upon it through an excavation to the upper air, though we dare not stand near enough the water's edge to get a glimpse of the blue sky far above. How very cold the water is, and what a curious, limy color! We never looked up a well before. A pole like a fishing rod lies near. The elder plumbs the depths, and all but a few inches disappears. Ugh! While from the rocks above and around, the drops of moisture fall into the tiny lake with a slow, solemn plash — plash. Now and then a horrible, icy drop falls upon our necks or hands. To think that human beings have slept in this cave! Why, we can't find an even surface large enough for a couch! They would die in such a charnel-house. Little Willie's nerves are by this time on the keen edge of desperation. Half ashamed but wholly in earnest, he puts in a plaintive little "please," and we escort him to the place of egress, give him a cheery word and up he goes the thirty-five feet of ladder like a squirrel, and is safe on *terra firma*. We, too, after waking the echoes, chipping off specimens, and exploring over the same territory, not daring to try a new "gallery," conclude that it is time for refreshments, and ascend ; but oh, what looking objects we are in the light of day! We express our skepticism in regard to this subterranean region ever having been used as a sleeping apartment. "Oh yes," we are assured, "and what is most remarkable, prisoners never took cold; and for a hundred years nothing has ever been known to mould down there."

With thanks for the courtesy begged for us and kindly extended to us, we take leave of the gentlemen.

"But," says the younger, "you'll want to know with whom you've been traveling all this time:" and there's a simultaneous fumbling in pockets all round for cards. Luckily we are provided, but judge our consternation on learning that our "college boy," is a business man some twenty miles away.

We hurry off to laugh over the *denouement.*

Now for lunch! "What did you put up, Lucy mine? A lot, I hope, for I am nearly famished."

"I put up? Why, I thought *you* put up! Didn't you?" (severely.)

Here's a predicament.

"Now, Marmee, there's another chance for the display of your superior tactics."

Over trots Marmee to the good woman across the way, and negotiates with her for oats for Billy, and a nice substantial farmer's meal for ourselves.

After demolishing the tempting viands, we turn our faces homeward, and, as children say in their composition, "very much pleased with our visit."

My School Children.

...

Daisy, the starry-eyed brunette,
The darling, and universal pet:
And freckled *Patsy*, the Irish rogue,
With his ready wit, and his comical brogue;
My saintly *Annie*, with eyes of blue,
And the soul of an angel looking through ;
And little blonde *Cora*, all white and red,
And a great, precocious, Websterian head ;
And down in the front, with a fool's cap on,
Sits the thick-headed and awkward *John*.
Proud little *Lizzie*, with nut-brown hair
And a style so dashing and debonaire :
And precious *Nellie*, I love so well,
For her face so calm and spirituelle :
And nervous *Auther*, never at rest,
Yet ranks 'mong his fellows first and best ;
Next *Eddie*, phlegmatic and lazy and fat,
Knowing naught but mischief, and stupid at that.
Poor, misnamed *Stella*, so hopelessly dull,
With her vacant face, and her empty skull ;

Rose, the purest of all my pearls,
And dear, meek *Lily*, with golden curls:
Irish *Denny*, the prodigy,
And *Tommie*, who will a statesman be!
Alice, the dusk, mulatto child,
With glistening teeth and elf-locks wild:
Dimpled *Maude*, with her hazel eyes,
In whose depths a world of witchery lies:
Willie, of rare, melodious voice,
In whose soaring song we all rejoice.
Poor, ragged *Tom*, well acquaint with dirt:
Belle, the little, incipient flirt:
Louise, of brilliant, glorious mind,
Within a casket plain enshrined:
And *Charlie*, a little German son,
The unconscious cause of lots of fun,
For his broken speech, so full of kinks,
And his ducking bows and his wicked winks:
And *Michael*, the careless, with unkempt hair,
As if he had never a mother's care.
So they gather, my children all,—
Gather, each morn, at the teacher's call,
The teacher—God help to be good and true,
My little darlings, to *all* of you.

                                              1871.

In the Class Room.

Then said the Leader, " What has Christ done for you? what is
He doing now? and what will He do for you?"

—— • • • ——

WHAT Christ hath done? I can not tell thee,
        brother ;
  I can not, in my poor thought, comprehend
All that great question : but I know none other
  Has ever proven such a wonderous friend.

Often, in meditation, I revolve it,
  As constant to my daily task I go ;
But it o'erwhelms me when I try to solve it,
  That He could love what is unlovely, so.

With some of earth, I might indeed dissemble —
  Might seem to be far better than I am —
Might possibly some fair ideal resemble,
  And still be but a miserable sham :

But Christ can pierce all masks and foolish seeming :
  From Him I can not hide a single blot ;

To any hideous stain that needs redeeming,
    Those searching, loving eyes are blinded not.

What *has* He done ? O, if I could but tell thee !
    I was a criminal, condemned to die ;
Guilty and wretched. But what grace befell me !
    He brought my pardon from the throne on high.

Infinite love ! I do not understand it ;
    It is a deep, unfathomable mystery ;
I only know the heart of God, who planned it,
    Found in Itself excuse, and not in me.

What *is* He doing ? Ah, to tell that story
    A tongue of inspiration must be given.
I can not tell thee, till in fields of glory
    My spirit is from earthly limits shriven.

I could as soon the myriad sea-sands number ;
    Or count the ocean drops, and tell their sum ;
Or call from mountain caves the winds that slumber ;
    But on this theme my lips seem stricken dumb.

I would be eloquent, and ever telling
    What Christ is doing for me every day—
What marvels He doth work ; and thus impelling
    Some other soul to choose this blessed way.

But somehow when my trembling lips are fashioned
  To speak, my words seem paralyzed and dead,
And cold, and meaningless, and unimpassioned,
  Compared with what I feel and *would* have said.

And so I can not tell thee what He 's doing,
  Altho' I long to break the silent spell :
But that dear love is all my heart imbuing,
  I 've sometimes brokenly essayed to tell.

What *will* He do?   Far more than I can mention,
  In Him my soul has never been deceived ;
And so I have of death no apprehension,
  Because I know Him whom I have believed.

But an under-current of sadness,
  Like a serpentine thread of pain,
Permeates all my gladness
  And joy in the Lamb that was slain.
What have I done for Jesus?
  For my years have not been few.
What am I doing at present ?
  And what do I mean to do ?

O, I do not want to die yet :
  I am not ready to go :
I can not see my sun set

Till I have some trophy to show—
Some faults overcome — some graces —
  Some bundle of ripened wheat —
Some jewel from desert places,
  To lay at the Master's feet:

Some soul from the brink of perdition,
  From trials sore brought through,
To testify my contrition
  Was genuine, deep and true.
O. if he comes ere morning,
  Is my record such an one —
If He comes with the solemn warning
  That my work is over and done ?
Alas! alas! I have only
  Taught the children day by day.
Have I sought the burdened and lonely,
  And kept them from going astray ?
I have prayed with my little people
  Each morn the long year through :
Have I been uniformly gentle,
  Impartial, tender and true ?
Have I loved the wayward and stubborn,
  As well as the undefiled ?
Have I tried, with divine compassion,
  To win the most wretched child ?
Looking beyond the external,
  Repulsive as it may be,

Have I loved them with love maternal,
  For Thee, dear Lord, for Thee?
And when I have, thoughtless, wandered
  Perhaps where the tempted stood,
Have I altogether squandered
  My chances for doing good?
Have I been to sister and brother
  All that I might have been,
Proving to them that none other
  But Christ can cleanse from sin?
Alas for the mournful story,
  Confessed with bitterest shame!
What hope can I have for glory,
  Although I have named His name?
But I can not go empty-handed
  Into Eternity—
Faithless, forever branded.
  Lord, give me souls for Thee.
O, if to-night I am summoned
  Before the eternal throne,
I can only cry to the Master,
  Saved—but by grace alone.

Ella.

... -

Bring flowers, white flowers, o'er the dead to strew,
Only pale flowers, and pure as the snow:
For one who was purer and sweeter than they,
Like a blossom, has faded from Earth away.

Fold a pale rose in her waxen palm:
No thorn will ruffle her solemn calm;
Scatter fresh buds round her fair young head:
They are meet, they are fit for the beautiful dead.

How like a bride, in her vestments white,
She looks to your tear-dimmed, tender sight,
Or like sculptured stone,—so passionless, cold
And still is the heart that her robes enfold!

Gaze on her features sublimely still,
No shadow of sorrow, no trace of ill,
Only a stately and grand repose,
Unmoved by humanity's joys or woes.

Linger yet lovingly round her clay,
Whence the saintly spirit has flown away:
Break not, poor heart, with bitter pain,
As you give back your darling to God again.

But a memory sweeter than stainless flower
Treasure forever, from this sad hour,
Of all her sweet graces, far more dear
Than the soulless tenement lying here.

She sleeps, O Sister! Not in your arms
Who would have shielded her from Earth's harms,
Not in her own dainty room,
And not in the desolate, lonely tomb.

She sleeps! To the Saviour's compassionate breast
He gathers His lamb to her heavenly rest:
O well may ye cease, sad eyes, to weep,
Because—" He gives His *beloved*—sleep!"

The Flower of the Holy Spirit.

In a sunny land afar,
On the Isthmus Panama,
Fed by tropic sun and shower,
Grows a strangely fashioned flower ;
Its corolla, cup-like, white,
Drinks the long day's torrid light,
Till it stands divinely fair
On its stalk, uplifted there.

Nestled in its deepest heart,
Is the strangest, loveliest part ;
There the inner petals fold
O'er the anthers' dusty gold,
And, as if to hint God's love,
Make a perfect snow-white dove :
So the Spaniards reverently
Christened it the *Fleur d'Esprit.*

Oh, my heart ! though storms assail,
Till the fibres cringe and quail ;

Though the fierce fires of despair
Wrap thee in their angry glare,
From their discipline at length
Thou shalt gather bloom and strength,
And a fitting temple be
For the heavenly *Fleur d'Esprit.*

12

Dulce Pro Mori.

...

Sweet to die and escape all pain,
Ceasing to toil for impossible gain,
Ceasing from rivalry, failure and tears,
Ignoble struggles and unworthy fears :
Sweet to lie down to an untroubled rest,
With Nature's green coverlet over the breast.

Never a call in the morning to wake,
With a burdened heart sinking and ready to break ;
Never a call to labor unpaid,
Never again to have trust betrayed,
Never to prove affection a lie,—
O 't would be sweet to lie down and die.

No more to work with head, heart and hands,
But to have thwarted our dearest plans ;
No more to wrestle with grief or sin,
The wrongs without and the evils within,—
O for that peaceful and dreamless sleep

Where hearts never ache and eyes never weep!
But sweeter to live and bravely endure,
To our own best instincts proving truer,
Resting in God with a holier faith
Than weakly to pray for the rest of death,—
Sweeter to live for humanity's sake,
Striving to cheer other hearts that ache.

Sweeter to live and *our* griefs ignore,
Ministering to others, sin-sick and sore,
Striving their woes to lighten or share,
Giving God's poor our best thought and care:
Thus our own troubles, before we think,
Will into insignificance sink.

Sweeter to live—but not for self,
Not for ambition, nor lore, nor pelf,
Nor aught that this world can offer man,
Hollow and false since the world began.
Yes! sweeter to live, and to do God's will
Till His Hand shall all our pulses still.

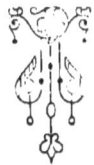

A Sick Room Lesson.

HER features, pinched and drawn with pain,
  Deep sunken eyes, and whitened hair—
A form, attenuate and thin :
  You recognize disease is there.

Disease, in gastly, sickening phase,
  Yet something more I recognize,—
Something in that poor, wasted face,
  And something in the hollow eyes.

That, like a steady, vestal flame,
  On consecrated shrine or pyre,
Quenchless and bright, nor dimmed by pain,
  Illumes her face with holy fire.

And thus it is no place of gloom :
  You could not think it sad, or drear,
This small, old-fashioned, homely room ;
  For there 's an angel brooding here ;

And Resignation is her name.
　She lights the fire in those old eyes:
And by some heavenly grace she turns
　To praise her pain-extorted cries.

I 'll take the goodly lesson home,
　To sanctify both heart and mind.
Come health or sickness, joy or gloom,
　To Jesus' will I 'll be resigned.

A Tribute of Love

To the Memory of the late Hattie L. Flower,
a Former Contributor of Zion's Herald.

• • •

I SEE her in the olden place,
   And can not think her dead :
The silvery curls about her face,
   And round her snowy head
Bleached white with pain, and not with time,
Wreathe aureoles of a frosty rime.

Because I always found her there,
   I can not make it seem,
That vacant room and empty chair,
   Aught but a troubled dream —
A grim and haunting midnight spell,
That morning sunshine will dispel.

Yes, still I see the hazel eyes
   Her countenance illume :
And think I find in mortal guise
   An angel in the room,

So heavenly sweet are her replies,
Her hope so sure beyond the skies.

I sit, and on her converse feed,
 And quite forget to go ;
For lofty sentiments indeed
 Forth from her bosom flow,
While I but dimly understand
Such Christian heights, sublimely grand.

The limits of one narrow room
 Enclosed her world for years :
Yet never word of doubt or gloom
 Fell upon watchful ears :
Nor loving eyes e'er knew her shed
Repining tears of shrinking dread.

Prone with disease and racking pain —
 The furnace fires for her —
Yet to the Christ-like spirit's gain
 All did but minister :
And He who made the Fourth of old,
Hath brought her through, refined as gold.

Her life seems one long sacrifice —
 'Gainst suffering no defense :
Yet hers a nature that would rise
 And triumph over sense.

Strong and sustained by God alone,
Abiding ever near His throne.

The discipline was sharp and long,
  Yet purer is the gem,
And sweeter is the seraph song —
  Brighter her diadem ;
For grace divine perfected thus
The rare sweet spirit gone from us.

As perfume on a summer wind
  Betrayeth blossoms near,
So fragrant memories left behind
  Cling round her name so dear :
And in our hearts, enshrined deep,
The treasure of that name we keep.

And still I can not, will not, think
  Of her as dead.   Ah, no !
From that sad, mournful word I shrink,
  It means so much of woe.
I think of her as glorified ;
I think of her as Heaven's bride.

Pictures.

...

A window, hung with costly lace,
 And through the draperies, I can see
A youthful mother's tender face,
 Her baby on her knee.

And both are clad with richest care :
 The room is large and warm and bright,
All luxuries of wealth are there,
 And 't is a pleasant sight.

A pleasant picture—yet I know
 That mother, fair and sweet and young,
Has her own secret, cankering woe,
 And oft her heart is wrung.

Nor babe, so bright and promising,
 Nor all that plenteous gold can buy,
Can from her heart abstract the sting,
 The sadness from her eye.

This is her grief,—and this her shame,—
    That she is a neglected wife:
Her husband's a dishonored name,
    And hers a blighted life.

Another picture I can see,
    A needle-woman, thin and wan,
Dwelling alone in penury,
    And youth and beauty gone.

                    .

The room is cold and bare and dim :
    Her slender fingers sadly worn,
Weaving her broideries out and in —
    Her life of hope is shorn.

A memory stirs her feeble heart :
    It sets her being all aglow :
It makes the long pent tear-drops start,—
    That dream of long ago.

A dream of love and hope and youth,
    Evokes she from the buried past,—
A fair, false dream of Manhood's truth,
    Too beautiful to last.

And wand'ring down a street obscure
    Into a school-room, I can look

Where children sit, with gaze demure,
　Intent on slate or book.

The teacher's form I can descry,
　With something still of girlish grace,
A proud, pale brow, a thoughtful eye,
　An intellectual face.

A noble mission hers : and yet
　It fills not all that woman's heart—
Her sun of love hath darkly set —
　So soon life's dreams depart.

And then I ask, Is friendship vain
　And hollow mockery indeed ?
What mean these lives of ceaseless pain,
　These hearts that always bleed ?

Then from some higher, nobler sphere,
　An answer unto me was given,
And this is what I seemed to hear :
　There 's nothing *true* but Heaven.

"He that Comforteth You."

———•••———

AND shall not that suffice for all the crosses
　　We bear, while journeying through this "vale
　　　　of tears?"
Shall not this compensate for all Earth's losses,
　　Hush our complainings, and dispel our fears?

When all the world has seemed a vain deceiving,
　　And those we trusted most have proved untrue,
O, let *this* silence all our selfish grieving:
　　"I, even I, am He that comforts you."

"I, even I," what heavenly condescension
　　The Lord of all the universe bestows!
Though I were crushed with grief, I 'd dare to
　　　　mention
　　Never again my petty, childish woes.

I do remember One — a man of sorrows,
　　With every phase of human grief acquaint.

And when I think of Him my sore heart borrows
  A holy comfort, and I do not faint.

Trustful and cheerful then, I bear my burdens—
  My Father knoweth best my spirit's need.
He hath assured me of celestial guerdons,
  He will my wandering feet in safety lead.

Afflictions, that had seemed too great and bitter,
  I know He sends, my weak heart to refine :
That for Heaven's purity I may be fitter,
    As grapes are bruised and crushed to yield us
        wine.

No longer will I mourn that He ordaineth
  This love and that be stricken from my life,
For God, I know, in tender mercy reigneth,
  And He will guard me from all needless strife.

Tender and true—but not like mortal lover,
  This is a pledge divine—tender and true—
I claim it always mine, till life be over,
  " I, even I, am He that comforts you."

Easter.

...

With precious ointment, and spice and myrrh,
  Three sorrowing women, at break of day,
Meet at the mouth of the Sepulchre—
  And lo! the stone hath been rolled away!

Stooping they look in the rock-hewn grave,
  And two bright figures, in angel guise,
Instead of their Lord in that burial cave,
  Meet their astonished and frightened eyes.

" Why seek ye the living among the dead ?
  Your Lord is risen—He is not here : "
Thus unto Mary the Angel said,
  In sweetest accent of heavenly cheer.

" Your Lord is risen ! " She turned and there
  Stood Jesus,—the Master—the Crucified.
" Mary ! " and calm grew her troubled air :—
  " Rabboni ! " the woman, responsive, cried :

" Rabboni ! "   And fell at her Master's feet.
    Wondering, loving, believing then :
  Her grief all turned to a joy complete,
    The joy of the ransomed Magdalene.

" The Lord is risen ! "   O, soul of mine,
    Mount skyward then as on angel wings !
  This message sing in your flight divine,
    Till the whole wide universe with it rings :

" The Lord *is* risen," this Easter day !
    Cease forever my tears to flow !
  I 'll chant his mercy and love alway
    Till home to my risen Lord I go !

The Cry of the Desolate.

• • •

O Lamb of God! Thou hast known all,
　All suffering and all frailties that we know,
All grievous trials which our souls befall,
　Life's every phase of weakness and of woe.

O Lamb of God! I cry to thee ;
　Crushed to the earth beneath each heavy cross,
In the worn spirit's dire extremity,
　Only the Heart divine can know my loss.

O Lamb of God! The broken reed
　I dared to lean upon, and trusted so
Proved but a bitter mockery indeed :
　Trembling and faint and weak, I let it go.

O Lamb of God! I found it clay,
　The idol in my deepest heart enshrined :
Now fallen into ruins and decay
　I cast the unworthy object from my mind.

O Lamb of God! All earth-born hopes,
  That were to me like flowers of Paradise,
Proved only perishable Passion flowers,
  And now have fallen to dust before my eyes.

O Lamb of God! There is life,
  A higher life, to which my soul aspires ;
Bereft of earthly hopes, weary of strife,
  I would renounce all worldly, weak desires.

Dear Lamb of God! O teach me resignation,
  Give me a firmer faith of hope and peace :
So shall I learn to shun each sore temptation,
  And calm and patient wait the soul's release.

"We All do Fade as the Leaf."

...

How fade the leaves? The frost and sun,
    Chemists of earth and skies,
Press out the summer's tender green,
    Press in all royal dyes :

Till all the forest flames and glows,
    And every shrub is seen
Wearing her fiery coronal,
    Like some barbaric queen.

Richer than Summer's gayest flowers,
    Or webs from Eastern looms,
Or Indian fabrics strangely bright,
    Or gorgeous Tropic blooms.

These wonderous leaves, so richly stained,
    As if with blood or wine,
Call ye this fading? then I pray
    Such fading may be mine.

When life shall ebb, and earth recede.
  O, I would fade like this,
Perfecting. ripening for the land
  Of everlasting bliss.

Nor grieve that this poor tenement
  Of perishable clay
Must, like all mottled, glowing leaves.
  So shortly know decay.

My New Watch.

...

Tick, tick, little Watch, what are you trying to
say ?
Time is flitting and flying; flying and flitting
away :
I strike off the winged minutes with my little, re-
lentless hand,
And then you 've so many minutes less to live in
this mortal land.

Tick, tick, little Watch, and what will you have
me do ?
O, well if you heed the lesson I 'm trying to teach
to you !
For every ill spent moment, though it be ever so
brief,
In the judgment day your tears shall fall, in vain
and bitter grief.

Tick, tick, little Watch, O change your dreary tune !
Ah, my little monotonous note will surely change
full soon !

For time will soon be ended — Eternity will begin,
What then, if these priceless moments have e'er
  been spent in sin.

Tick, tick, little Watch, you prosy little thing !
I did not ask a sermom, I 'd rather hear you sing !
I only sing to the good and true, who use the
  moments well,
Who 've not to blush for squandered time — Are
  you one of those, pray tell ?

In Memory of Dog Tiger,

WHO DIED AT HILL FARM, OCTOBER, 1873.

Good-bye, old Tige, good-bye!
It may be weakness—yet
We grieve that he must die,
The dear old clumsy pet.
The tumbling, huge old hulk.
The noble Mastiff friend.
Death claims his mammoth bulk,
Old Tige is near his end.

Associations dear
Cling round his savage name,
Linked in with year on year,
Since first to us he came:
Grave, reverend, dignified,
His most becoming mood:
Manners that ne'er belied
His high, patrician blood.

Loving, intelligent,
.And vigilant, and brave,
Sagacious—yet content
   To be your friend, or slave.
Interpreting your look,
   If it be dark or bright :
.A frown he can not brook.
   A smile his heart's delight.

That " open countenance,"
   That happy wag of thine,
Old dog. what can enhance
   The gifts that in thee shine !
Beneath his shaggy coat.
   Full many virtues hide
We never thought to note
   (Like men) until he died.

Hero of many a battle.
   Comrade in many a play,
Guardian of herded cattle.
   Sentinel night and day,
Defending home and treasure,
   With staunch fidelity,—
In woodland romp and pleasure,
   Who half so gay as he ?

No more he'll chase the chickens
   That scatter panic struck,
Nor play the very dickens
   With waddling goose or duck.
No woodchuck, sleek and fat,
   In forest wide and dark,
Nor squirrel, coon, or cat,
   Need fear his valiant bark.

No more we hear a whacking
   Of that expressive tail,
No more the midnight barking
   That makes the robber quail.
His awkward gambols cease ;
   The almost human eye
Glazes with age, apace,—
   Good-bye, old dog, good-bye.

I wonder if a heaven
   Somewhere there may not be,
Which, after death, is given
   To faithful brutes like thee,—
Some wild and free domain,
   Some happy hunting ground,
Where large and toothsome game
   And roast beef bones are found ?

Only a soulless brute,
  Only a dog, you say !
But now his bark is mute,
  And he a lump of clay.
Blame not the saddened heart
  That prompts the chastened tear,
And feels a genuine smart
  O'er dear old Tiger's bier.

The self-made sexton Tim
  Will scoop his narrow bed,
Whistling a negro hymn
  O'er royal Tiger's head.
The winds chant sweet and low,
  And childishly we cry,
As slowly home we go,
  Good-bye, old Tige, good-bye.

Bob.

WRITTEN FOR A BOY.

— ••• —

Poor little, winsome Bob!
And I almost heard a sob
That pretty Bobbie cat should have to die.
And Teddie's nose is red,
And he turns away his head
To hide the mist that gathers in his eye.

Who killed our kitty cat?
Did he dine off too much rat
And a fit of indigestion prove enough?
Or some bad wicked boy
Teddie's little puss destroy,
By introducing him to pizen stuff?

Once in a pan of milk
Did he plunge with coat of silk,
When fleeing from a dreadful terrier,
And there he growled and spit:

Doggie never cared a bit,
And condescended not to wink or stir.

But Missis fished Bob out,
As an angler would a trout,
And dried him so he did 'nt take a cold.
Milk baths, they say, are good
For complexions and for food,
But Bobbie his opinion never told.

But Bob is heard no more
Galloping across the floor,
Chasing Teddie with a string or whip or spool,
With yellow eyes so bright,
And his furry feet so light,
Turning somersets — the funny little fool!

Papa the coffin gave,
And he dug a tiny grave,
And Teddie, as chief mourner, marched ahead:
I think o'er many a bier
There is mourning less sincere
Than for our little bob-tailed pussy, dead.

"A Dream

THAT WAS NOT ALL A DREAM."

——— • ◆ • ———

THE Editor sat in his easy chair
    With spectacles on his nose,
And his countenance lost its look of care,
While dozing and nodding; around him there
    Twelve cycles of time uprose.

Twelve years, that seemed forgotten and dead,
    Marched softly in at the door;
All lovingly gathered about his head,
And tender and beautiful things they said,
    Pertaining to days of yore.

He stirred uneasily once or twice,
    But the magical spell was deep,
And they held him long in a friendly vise,
Then disappearing all in a trice,
    The Editor woke from sleep.

"GLAD TO SEE YOU!" he roared aloud,
  And proved with a grip of iron ;
But whether to me or the vanishing crowd,
As he stood on the threshold happy and proud,
  Guess, oh ye brothers in Zion !

New Town Hall.

... ---

THERE was a noble motto,
　　Far in the days of old,
Held by the ancient Latins,
　　A people brave and bold :
And down upon the current
　　Of centuries ago,
Comes floating that old watchword,
　　" *Pro bono publico!* "

The nations of the Cæsars,
　　With all their classic braves,
Their grand historic heroes,
　　Sleep, in forgotten graves.
But *this* has well survived them,
　　This thought, so long agó
Breathed by some fine old Roman,
　　" *Pro bono publico!* "

And so shall stand this structure
　　We dedicate to-night,

When they whose hands upreared it,
    Shall all have passed from sight :
A monument enduring,
    Our Town Hall shall have stood,
To philanthropic spirits
    Who loved the public good.

Their names were never carven
    Upon Fame's dusty scroll,
And soon may be forgotten,
    As generations roll.
Yet these same names are fragrant
    To us who gather here,
With kind associations,
    And memories fond and dear.

For instance, who so quickly
    All turbulence will quell,
External or internal,
    As our beloved *Bell ?*
And in all public measures,
    We care not what betide,
We 'll stem all opposition,
    If (*W*)*right* is on our side !

Then, well and widely valued,
    To solace lonely hours,
We count among our treasures

A multitude of *Flowers.*
"Slow-blooming," says some cynic,
Wanting to criticise,
Not knowing Autumn blossoms
Have ever richest dyes.

Choice things in little parcels,
They sell at *Freeland's* store,
And that must be the reason
We like a *little Moore.*
And then with all the labor,
And toil in Life's rough ways,
How *should* we ever prosper
Without our *Hallidays?*

Our *Millers* and our *Gaylords*
To foreign parts were sent,
But have we not among us
Our own good Duke of *Kent?*
And for housekeeper's uses,
High on our list we put
What none will undervalue,
Our much esteeméd *Root.*

Of petrified old fogies,
The town has had enough!
Of animated mummies,
And other worthless stuff.

But when we need a servant
    Some public trust to fill,
Devoted, staunch, and faithful,
    We 'll re-elect *Churchill !*

And now, the months reviewing,
    That, steadily on high
Brick after brick has risen,
    Triumphant toward the sky,
Till school, and hall, and turret,
    Shapely and fair we see,
'T is fitting that we gather
    In festive jubilee.

Perchance there are some grumblers
    Who " want it understood
They voted strong agin it ;
    It won't do them no good ;"—
The times demand such fossils
    Be laid upon the shelf !
Too late, this age, for living
    Exclusively for self.

We need not fear to cherish
    Too much of patriot zeal ;
Large-hearted and true manhood
    Will serve the public weal ;

14

Will bind upon his frontlet
Wherever he may go,
That ancient Roman watchword,
" *Pro bono Publico!* "

1874.

"He Opened Not His Mouth."

O, if I could remember,
    Wincing 'neath some rude thrust,
That seems unduly cruel,
    Malignant and unjust—
Some word that makes indignant
    The blood to finger-tips—
O, if I could remember
    He opened not his lips.

When some old ghost, well hidden
    And buried out of sight,
I think past resurrection,
    Is sudden dragged to light
By hands of Goth and Vandal,
    Unsparing, merciless,—
O, if I could remember
    He deadliest foes could bless.

When so-called friends ungently
    Touch some old cicatrice,

O, that exquisite anguish —
　　Betrayal with a kiss;
That keenest edge of suffering
　　I dimly apprehend,
Yet ken not how the Master
　　Addressed him still as "friend."

O, if I could remember,
　　When provocations come,
Jesus, accused all falsely,
　　E'en like a lamb was dumb,
He answered not, and meekly
　　Received the crown of thorn;
I turn in hot resentment,
　　And hurl back scorn for scorn.

He, grieved, despised, insulted
　　By fierce and angry men,
Scourged, mocked with bitter railing,
　　Reviled not back again;
I strive, alas! all vainly,
　　To teach th' unconquered will
That meek and Christly lesson,
　　To suffer and be still.

O, if I could remember
　　No venomed barb can fall,
No polished shaft of malice,

But Jesus sees it all,
And lovingly invites me
    Upon His heart to lay
Each burden, great or trivial,
    Forever and alway.

Letter from Martha's Vineyard.

— ••• —

MARTHA'S VINEYARD, August, 1875.

YES, Mr. Editor, that quartette of teachers before alluded to in your columns have shuffled off professional primness, laid aside the character of hard task-mistress over "dapper little lads and rosy lassies," and have flown away to the sea on a regular teacher's spree. Sitting on deck, as we approach the Island, we discern a bold bluff whose base is kissed by the frolicking waves, and whose summit is crowned with countless cottages, dainty and fanciful enough in design for the homes of woodland elves and fairies. Momently it rises clearer, outlining itself with minute distinctness against the sapphire background of sky. And now a strain of music, delicious band music, welcomes the steamer from the Sea View House. Pleasant recognition greets three of our number. Your correspondent looks into strange faces only, but by great grace and clemency the quartette remains unbroken, and we are all domiciled under one roof. Like Dickens' Little Joe, we feel to exclaim,

"I 'm in luck, I am!" as we are escorted to the Loomis cottage on Ocean avenue by its genial and gentlemanly proprietor.

And then from its upper balcony, we look out upon that incomparable view of the ocean, and for a space are dumb with admiration. Not for long. We burst into rhapsodies. We exhaust our adjectives. We realize as never before that our command of language is too beggarly for such a scene as this. If we only had acres of canvas, and could dip our brush in a rainbow, Mr. Editor, we 'd paint it for you: A magnificent stretch of sea, laughing and dimpling in the sunshine, flecked with from two to three hundred sails. Some in the foreground, standing out full-sized, majestic and beautiful, every detail of mast and rope and spar clear-cut as an exquisite pencilling, the brilliant high-lights and deep Rembrandt shadows of the sails eclipsing every *chef-d'œuvre* of the "old masters" as nature must always eclipse art, and some in dim perspective, far on the horizon line, like the phantom ship in Coleridge's Ancient Mariner. An ever moving panorama! a vision that never cloys!—this heaving, surging, moaning sea, with her freight of brigs and schooners floating on to parts unknown, with her low-browed, ugly, but practical, steamers, and her pleasure barks with parti-colored pennons, lovely, if not as costly, as Cleopatra's barge. Even a call to supper from our large-hearted hostess (for she chooses to make us "company" to-day) does

not break the spell. That ocean view, like the Irish-
man's rum, is "victuals, drink and lodging" to us, till
we are assured that the view is warranted to keep; and
then one demure little damsel confessed to a feeling of
"wentness." (Do n't be scandalized, oh editor! Last
term we felt quite in the "sere and yellow leaf;" but
we 've lost a dozen years to-day, and are enthusiastic
school girls again, brimming with gush—and slang)—
so we went gladly.

The days are full of delights. We realize the Italian
dolce far niente, and become unconscionably lazy. We
sail, fish, bathe, eat and drink, and are merry, and in the
twilight sit and gloat over our sea view. There 's inspiration in every breeze, only we feel inspired to do nothing but dream. It is a land of enchantment, and its
glamour is over us all.

Tuesday morning there 's a challenge to action:
"Come, girls, ho for Nantucket!" And after rehears-
ing the well-worn Indian legend of how Nancy took it,
to three young ladies in two rooms, sitting up on elbow
in bed, and firing the imaginations of our hearers by re-
lating all we know, and some things we do n't, about the
place, dressing up the latter in our most attractive style,
they are prevailed upon reluctantly to rise and equip
themselves for the expedition;—an act attended by some
haps and mishaps, whereby hangs a tale, of which
"coffee," lost to the world, is the key-note. Breathless,
we reach the steamer "Island Home," and embark, with

one cuff off and one cuff on, like "my son John," in our favorite author, Mother Goose. A leisurely two hours' sail takes us across the intervening twenty-eight miles. Once we are almost out of sight of land—only the dimmest blue line in the distance betokens terra firma.

As we near the quaint and picturesque old town, we crowd forward eagerly. It is all huddled together, with snug compactness, and the remainder of the island is a barren sandbank, rising abruptly out of the sea. Two of us mount chairs, and under pretense of scanning the landscape, skyscape and waterscape, peer furtively into the pilot-house, where are two of the ship's officers and the man at the wheel. "Oh none of that, girls," says another, rebuking their traditional woman's curiosity: "you need n't try to sugar them over! They won't look at you!" One of the officers smiles indulgently and whispers, "You can come in here when you come back." Now on the door of this apartment was written, in offensively large characters, "No admittance." Therefore, we set this down as another act of great grace and clemency, whereof we were the subjects.

Bounding Sankaty light-house we are soon in port, and have chartered a crazy old carryall with a juvenile charioteer to show us about the town. Up hill and down we are driven; through shell-paved streets, so narrow, neighbors in opposite windows can almost shake hands across. The houses, mostly ancient, are shingled not on

the roof alone, but all over, and bearing some lingering
vestiges of paint, generally red paint, as that withstands
the action of the salt air best.   We visited the oldest
house, built in 1686, where are shown mammoth sea tur-
tles, etc.; climbed the Old South Tower (and repented for
a week after), where a watchman is stationed at night to
give alarm in case of fire, and where the eye commands a
view of the whole island; saw the bell-man going about
the streets ringing out his announcement of lecture or
concert in primeval style; laughed at the awkward two-
wheeled, one-horse carts with a step behind, in which
the *elite* of the place take their airings; dined at an old-
fashioned country hotel, and gossiped with various people.   "The young folks all leave the place," said one gar-
rulous old body; "nobody left but us old folks now;
become extinct pretty soon."   "But what do you live
on, business seems so stagnant?"   "Live on each other,
sorter.   Then there 's a good many retired sea captains,
too cautious to invest their money in any thing new."
The wharves, all gone to decay, a mass of debris level
with the water, tell how the place has fallen from its
pristine glory.   We looked on, not in speculative mood
only, for it had a mournful sort of historic interest for
us, since certain of our kin, a tall and handsome com-
mander of a whaler, sailed always from this port, and
won here his Quaker-born wife, the elegance and polish
of whose manners and the richness of whose *trousseau*
were admired beyond the limits of this poor and lonely

little island. Dead, now:—dead, too, and forever departed, the business life and activity that once pulsated through the streets of this venerable Quaker town. On board the steamer again, and dutifully scribbling a postal home, we are graciously informed that we may be admitted into the coveted *sanctum* sanctorium—the pilot-house. The gallant captain and mate are most entertaining. We feel a little shy of the former on account of his superior position and our ignorance, but he condescendingly lays aside his dignity, and binnacle, compass and spy-glass are laid under contribution for our enlightenment. Sailors' yarns are reeled off to our vast delectation; and I suppose those two urbane gentlemen have n't refreshed themselves with the sight of four greater little fools this many a day than your quartette of teachers. We look in the bronzed faces of those two sons of Neptune with ill-disguised admiration while they answer our questions, wise and otherwise (mostly the latter, we suspect), in regard to navigation, bell-buoys, the telegraphic cable laid from the main land to the Vineyard, etc., *ad infinitum*, while an occasional *jeu d'esprit*, like a rocket, flashing out from the lips of Martha (not the legendary Martha of the Vineyard), the wit of the company, makes the little pilot-house ring with our merriment. Well, there 's an end to all sublunary things, and so there is an end to our lessons in navigation from our patient and eminently able instructors, Capt. Manter and Mate Fitzgerald of the steamer

Island Home. But we shall not soon forget the marked courtesy and kindness extended to us on board their boat. "Girls," said one, confidentially, "I think we can safely set that down as a compliment;" and so it was received with a great deal of unexpressed exultation. Such a lot of Westfieldians at the Vineyard, and all as "happy as a clam at high tide!" (If nautical quotations abound hereafter, please attribute it to— any thing you please). And scarcely a Springfield face. How it is that the people of Springfield so ignore this gem of sea-side resorts is a problem too deep for our solving. Its attractions can scarcely be paralleled, certainly not surpassed. Katama and South Shore are in reserve for us, a future day; likewise Gay Head, twenty-five miles distant, with its many-colored rocks of curious geological formation. A short cruise to Cape Poge is the programme for to-morrow. If we "fish for a whale and catch it," you shall be duly informed, though we shan't feel to grumble if we take a seventeen-pound blue fish, as did one of our neighbors recently. Time forbids just now any reference to the camp-ground, and a thousand things that demand notice. We go now to feast our eyes again on the sublime spectacle of old ocean stretching for countless leagues away, and so, perchance, more anon.

Eleventh Anniversary.

—‥•◆•——

As mothers love to celebrate
 Each natal day returning,
Of all their darlings, small or great,
 With partial fondness yearning,
So comes Dame Trinity to-day,
 Her outspread arms caressing·
The Mission Child that came last May,
 And gives the bairn her blessing.

Like Samuel, child of many prayers,
 Had been the embryo Mission,
Through years of waiting, toils and cares,—
 At last came glad fruition.
At last the old North Main Street Class,
 Through struggles agonizing,
The grand finale brought to pass,
 An infant church uprising.

That good old Class of '64,
 What memories round it hover!

'T is well to glance its annals o'er.
  And live its triumphs over.
There, spiritual pabulum
  Invariably sat good,
On saint and sinner, old and young,
  Administered by Atwood.

And now, in 1875,
  We boast what can 't be beaten.
A Sunday School that 's all alive.
  Because — it 's "run" by Eaton.
A Bible Class enthused with brain,
  Whose virtues next would I sing,
(Our loss is our pet Mission's gain).
  Conducted by one Rising!

These are but lesser lights, we know,
  Round their grand center paling;
The master mind to whom we owe
  Allegiance unfailing.
Our Pastor! few the flocks indeed
  That such a prize inherit;
The Church's pride, the Mission's need!
  Hulburd! well christened Merritt!

One year ago a goodly throng
  Within these walls assembled,

Then first they echoed to a song,
    And 'neath a sermon trembled.
Brown were the rafters—cobwebbed o'er—
    Rude and unsightly may be,
(Rude as the manger that of yore
    Enshrined a heavenly Baby !)

But willing hands had polished well
    Rough floor, and beam, and rafter,—
And still the brethren love to tell
    Of *one*, mid smothered laughter,
Prefiguring them that walk in *white*,
    Yet armed with nail and mallet,
Who like a Trojan wrought that night,
    Our chronic joker — Hallet !

That snowy drapery fluttering free !
    Some, still, perchance may doubt it !
But "thereby hangs a tale," you see —
    Ask Atwood all about it !
Tired hands, but happy hearts next morn,
    Spirits that wearied never,
Beheld the Christian project born
    Of patient, long endeavor !

And God's sweet sunshine fell as bright
    As if through stained glass sifted,

And angels leaned to view the sight
  Of souls to Christ uplifted;
Here, in this strange, unwonted place
  So humble, and so lowly,
Here shone the mystery of God's grace
  On that May Sabbath holy.

The oriole in the apple tree
  Hushed his roulade and listened,
And turned his pretty head to see
  The Ringgold Mission christened.
The bees hummed sleepily and low
  Outside the rustic casement,
And robin with his breast aglow
  Looked on in mute amazement.

While hymn and skyward mounting prayer
  In solemn dedication,
Floated like incense on the air
  From priest and congregation,
And worldly hearts unused to pray,
  And wandering far from Heaven,
Were somehow strangely touched that day,
  And won to God that even.

So all the records of the year
  Repeat the blessed story;

You 've marked the penitential tear,
  And heard the shout of glory,
And this to some is holy ground —
  Tread reverently, brother,
So dear a spot the wide earth round
  Holds not for them another.

Then go thee forth our first-born one,
  Our dearly cherished Mission,
We 'll bear thee up to Heaven's throne,
  On many a fond petition.
Thy flock an undivided whole!
  No heresy or schism
Divide thee, as the years shall roll
  Far from the May-day chrism.

But peace, and harmony, and love,
  And holy Christian union,
And gracious influence from above,
  Cement thy saints' communion;
Till meet our noble Mission bands
  In fields forever vernal —
In temples builded not with hands,
  High in the heavens eternal.

15

Watch Night.

— •••

THE last hour of the gray old year!
  In silent prayer, on bended knee
O'er follies past we drop a tear,
  And wait, O Lord, on Thee.

From many a pit-fall, many a snare,
  Thy love alone hath kept our feet:
Our hearts are touched by Thy kind care,
  So infinitely sweet.

How near to awful moral wreck,
  Or dangers physical we 've been,
We know not: but some timely check
  Of Thine hath saved from sin.

For mercies rich and numberless,
  That all the changeful year have crowned,
Our Father's glorious name we bless,
  And loud His praises sound.

Some broken idol we bemoan :
  Some hopes lie buried 'neath the sod ;
And here Thy chastening hand we own,
  And bend us to Thy rod.

Millions and millions sleep to-day.
  Who, but one year ago to-night,
With health and happiness were gay.
  And looked toward futures bright.

Still our probation lingers yet !
  But when some year is growing old,
The sun upon our graves will set :
  Our story will be told ;

We shall have crossed life's troubled sea,
  And anchored on an unknown shore.
O, take us then to dwell with Thee,
  Dear Lord, for evermore.

A Prayer for the Poor.

Angels, pity all the poor!
Those who beg from door to door;
Those who tread with weary feet
Country lane, and city street:
Those whose faces pinched and pale.
Tell of want a woeful tale—
Tell of wretchedness and woe,
Such as but the poor can know.
Children shivering in the cold.
Faces prematurely old,
Little limbs so poorly clad;
Mothers! you would think it sad
Looked your petted darlings thus.
Pitiful appear to us
Tattered rags and hungry eyes,
Pleading lips and shuddering sighs,
Of the homeless squalid poor,
Begging thus from door to door.
Other worn and weary feet

Tread the cold, unfriendly street;
Men and women, grim and gaunt,
Victims of the demon Want—
O, what dire temptations lure,
Thinking of what they endure,
Thinking, sadly, as they must,
"Is the God above them just?"
Thinking madly, He, indeed,
Cares not for their bitter need,
Tempted thus, and tried so sorely,
Driven to despairing hourly;
O, what wonder if they faint,
And, ignoring all restraint,
Hopeless of a better time,
Reckless plunge them into crime,
Filching, then, from door to door!
Angels, pity all the poor!
Others tread the city street,
Amply shod their dainty feet;
Costly raiment wraps them round,
Blessings rare their lives have crowned;
They are sumptuously fed,
While a brother starves for bread.
Purse-proud, stiff-necked, unrefined,
Coarse and groveling heart and mind,
Yielding no allegiance to
That good God who blessed them so;
Never beg they at your door,

Yet they 're pitiably poor —
Poorer far than any other.
E'en the starved and ragged brother.
Men with natures warped and mean.
Men whose lives with vices teem.
Narrow-souled and sordid men.
O, good angels! pity them!
Women, bound by golden fetters.
Who in ignorance snub their betters;
Flaunt abroad their shoddy dresses,
And their bought-and-paid-for tresses!
Slaves to one o'er-mastering passion,
Bow they at the shrine of fashion:
In the vortex, sinking lower,
Angels! pity all the poor.

A Church Member.

— ••• —

SHE sank on the pew's soft cushions,
    And drew off a dainty kid,
That the gems upon her fingers
    Perhaps might not be hid!
She shook out a cobweb kerchief,
    With its cloud of perfume sweet,
And was ready now in the temple
    Her Master and Lord to meet!

Her hands were ablaze with jewels,
    And round her neck they shone,
And each fair wrist was circled
    With a glittering golden zone.
A luminous diamond dew-drop,
    Pendant from either ear,
Glowed like a dancing sunbeam
    Frozen into a tear.

One precious, beautiful emblem
    Upon her breast she wore—

A cross—an elegant trinket,
  The heaviest cross she bore!
Up rose the pale young preacher.
  And "let us pray," he said;
My lady bowed devoutly,
  With air and mien well-bred.

A missionary sermon
  Announced the preacher then.
Nor suffered chronic slumberers
  To doze or nod again.
A dash of indignation
  Mixed with his words of zeal,
His eloquence compelling
  Their stubborn hearts to feel.

"Four hundred millions of heathen
  Reach out their eager hands
For the bread of life, the gospel,
  In their benighted lands.
Thousands of Bible-readers
  To India might be sent.
If this, my sisters, *only*
  Your jewelry were spent.

"Immortal souls are starving:
  And do you even heed

A CHURCH MEMBER.

The piteous plaint ascending,
    In your insatiate greed?
Wrapt in your selfish garments,
    A Pharisaic robe,
Have ye done aught to lessen
    The sins that belt the globe?

" For O, your tastes are morbid,
    And false and vain your pride;
Luxurious ease enthralls you,
    Unhallowed wants, beside;
Unworthy aims are cheating
    The Master of His due;
Women of Methodism,
    Sad is the charge, but true!

" O, would our Christian women
    With but devotion meet,
Strip off their senseless baubles,
    And cast them at His feet,
To whom belongs the treasure
    Of earth and mine and sea,
How long before the nations
    To Him would subject be?

" The gold that now bedizens
    Dear woman's lovely form,

Would send the truth to millions—
   Would feed, and clothe, and warm.
Would civilize, enlighten,
   And leaven soon the whole—
Would give the world salvation,
   From tropic to the pole."

My lady sat and pondered:
   Herself, for once, forgot:
Through all that peacock splendor
   The random arrow shot,
Nor dreamed the modest marksman
   Where struck the winged dart—
How torpid was the conscience—
   How cold the wordling's heart.

Complacent airs all vanished;
   A blush of tardy shame
Crept up her haughty features,
   And dyed her cheeks like flame.
With soul so sadly humbled,
   She dared not even pray.
One devotee of fashion,
   At least, went home that day.

For, though her only idol
   Was style and gorgeous dress,

Her all-embracing error,
　Consummate selfishness,
Her name was on the church-books —
　Of Methodism, too!
And " over true" the picture,
　Dear sister, was it you?

Centennial Jottings, 1876.

...

"THEE won't ever be sorry thee came?" and gentle
Friend Rebecca looked tranquilly on us, out of eyes undimmed by seventy-eight years of sight-seeing in this
world of wonders. "Why, it's a whole liberal educa-
tion!—I would n't miss it for a small fortune," we
burst out, something like a beer-bottle that must effer-
vesce a little to save an explosion, for we are full to the
brim of the marvels and glories of the Exposition. The
treasures of the world—the world of nature and art—
are here in such richness and lavishness that any ex-
travagance of speech seems impossible. If one could
take it all in, and retain, and assimilate, what a walking
encyclopedia one might become!

Here one gets more vivid impressions of national character in a moment than could be obtained in weeks of
reading. Witness the grotesque and fantastic, if not
horrible, carvings of serpents and dragons and feasts,
possible and impossible, on various contributions by pagan
countries, and contrast with them the geometrical de-

signs, and the carvings of flower and fern and fruit em-
ployed in the architecture and ornamentation of civilized
nations.

Here, too, one may delight his eyes on a thousand
things that even extended travel would not afford; as,
for instance, the crown jewels of Austria would hardly
be exposed to the common herd, who may here behold
their fac-simile, in size and color and variety, if not in
brilliance and value; a very handsome display it is, too.
We pay one minute's tribute to this sign of royalty, and
pass on to see the largest opal in the world. Unset, and
but partly cut, as large as a lady's palm, it lies with its
glowing heart of fire dimly traceable beneath the surface.
Briefly we linger before the gems of the great diamond
merchants, Tiffany, Starr and Marcus, and Caldwell.
Oh! those precious stones! Strange thoughts, that
nothing else in the great exhibition has wakened, float
through the brain as we gaze; thoughts of a city that
seems like a dream — a walled city, with gates. Beauty
and splendor unconceived are there. Amethyst and
emerald, jacinth and sapphire, sardonyx and beryl, gar-
nish the foundation of the wall — a jasper wall — and
every gate a single pearl. "And there shall in no wise
enter into it any thing that defileth, or worketh abomi-
nation, or maketh a lie." But our day-dreams are frag-
mentary and changing as the views in a kaleidoscope.

Here is the Russian cloth of gold. Fancy the nobles
and princes of a monarchy in such vesture, on occasion

—a literal golden armor! But while we pause, a memory, long buried under the deposit of years, comes to the surface. A bevy of school girls in the history class, and their beloved Miss Bliss enriching the prosy recitation with the story of Philip Second of Burgundy, dressed in cloth of gold, dying on a field of battle, which ever after was called, "the Field of the Cloth of Gold." Now, how plaguesome it is that no more returns! Was it in the days of the Plantagenets, when England made such a fuss over some little French provinces? And did Philip's vanity so blind him that he forgot that such garmenture would make him a "bright and shining mark" for the enemy? No use! Memory sullenly refuses to aid; we'll appeal to the books, or better, to Miss Bliss, that feminine epitome of history, ancient and modern, who, to this day, is the center of revolving satellites in the class-room.

The gold plate next attracts the eye. Nothing richer than solid silver for table furniture, has heretofore fallen under our unsophisticated notice, and we confess to being the least bit subdued, not to say stunned, by the massive magnificence of this gold plate, engraved with the most exquisite artist fancies. We are told that the precious metal is plated on bronze, and we heave a sigh of relief, for the sense of so much grandeur was decidedly oppressive. Another memory is waked up in a long unvisited corner of the brain—how, rambling once among the falling chestnuts, a gentleman related that when he was

received at the Russian court, the banquet tables were
spread with gold plate. It seemed like a fairy tale then,
and we fancied he colored the narrative a bit to astonish
the country hill-side frolickers, that autumn day; but
lo! here it is a verity, and we make our quondam friend
this tardy amends.

By and by, the educational department of Boston,
Cincinnati and Indianapolis throws us into transports of
delight. Such drawings and penmanship! Such neat-
ness and method, such pretty fancies, in original designs,
by little lads and lassies! Such examination papers!
"Oh," but you say, "there are errors *there*." Oh,
what is that to one who is accustomed to hearing, "A
valley is an elongated depression," rendered "long-
gaited desperation;" and to such statements as that
"Brazilian forests are filled with all kinds of monkeys,
and *other* beautiful birds;" and that the "Southern
States yield cotton, tobacco, and *other* delicious fruits!"
But for mechanical execution, and for the development
of taste and skill, these volumes of common school work
seem marvels of excellence, till a clergyman's wife from
Ohio informs us that "there is no reason why they should
n't, etc. Scholars and teachers just 'crammed' for Cen-
tennial, devoting many months almost exclusively to drawing and writing!" Notwithstanding our vehement ad-
vocacy of drawing, our enthusiasm drops to zero.

Here and there we pause a minute before the peas-
ant groups, in national costume, that transport us across

seas to Sweden, or Lapland, or some other "furrin part," not likely to be visited by us in any other manner. A party of ladies and gentlemen are also loitering by, having just passed the Swiss clock-mender. They approach an officer. He is tall, statuesque, motionless, after the fashion of his kind when in repose. Evidently in abstracted mood, he does not perceive that he is the subject of admiring remark. " Why. it 's a policeman, is n't it ? How perfect!" Unlike many of the treasures here, he is unticketed, " Do not handle ; " and one lady, with a view to turning him round for better inspection, steps airily forward, and takes hold of him. He leaps into the air ; she recoils with a terrified scream ; and the rest are convulsed with laughter, the policeman presently enjoying the situation most of all. Neither was it a nice piece of acting on his part, his duties being so mechanical that he may often lose himself in reverie amid the throng. Such scenes are said to have been repeated to the vast amusement of one party, and the corresponding chagrin of the other.

How shall we dare to speak of the treasures of Memorial Hall ? Yet it would seem that the veriest tyro might soon learn to discriminate with some justice, since there are such marked specimens of merit and of demerit. True, one wonders how some of the pictures, where the most common rules of perspective are violated, ever ran the gauntlet of criticism to get in here. Here is one with the shadows falling in two opposite directions, indicating that the artist (?) conceived of two suns in the heavens. But there's plenty to feed the æsthetic nature, without harrowing up the soul with the works of such an erratic genius. Here is one, where the dew lies on the grass so fresh, so natural, that you, on your tired pedestals, almost envy the barefoot cow-boy luxuriating in it. Another, where such life is given to flesh tints, such rotundity to limbs, that it seems as if the figures might almost step from their frames. Here is one — the Iron-worker.

The scene is the throne-room of a palace. The king, in crown and regal robes, stands on the platform, with commanding mien, confronting an angry and excited crowd. One arm is outstretched toward the occupant of the throne, a bronzed and stalwart Vulcan of a fellow, a toiler in some lowly sphere, his shirt-sleeves shoved above the elbow. He sits with folded arms, dignified, calm, the only one unmoved. The others, by every fierce and frantic gesticulation and expression, manifest their scorn, malice, contempt, ridicule, disappointment and impotent rage at the situation. We grope a little, and then a fragment of a story from the Talmud dawns on us, with half uncertain ray — how king Solomon once pledged his throne to the most useful worker in metals ; and they came, the silversmith and the goldsmith and the worker in precious gems, and all the hungry horde of self-seekers ; but the wise man's decision fell on the brawny blacksmith — the iron-worker.

16

A tiny bit of canvas near by is called, "The old clock on the stairs," and it seemed as if the pensive, silver-haired old lady in the picture was keeping time with the click of her knitting needles to the solemn, monotonous

> " Forever — never !
> Never — forever ! "

of the tall, quaint clock on the stair-landing of this

> "Old-fashioned country-seat
> Somewhat back from the village street."

It was easy to live over with her the scenes of the poem. There were the stairs down which the bride tripped

> "On her wedding night ; "

and in that

> " Room below
> The dead lay in his sheet of snow."

Dear old lady, sitting there alone, sweet, patient and saintly, one longed to break in on the old clock's half sad, half glad refrain, with a burst of sympathetic

> " Earth hath no sorrow which Heaven can not heal."

Strange what power in a few feet of canvas to move the soul !

Often it was with an effort that visible emotion was restrained, for in this proper throng one would n't be guilty of "gush," nor of making a "scene." But when standing before Murillo's Christ it was necessary to summon the stern sentinel Will, to keep the gate of the tears

fast shut, so vivid, so intense was the unutterable agony
in that countenance so human, so divine. The tenderness without weakness, the strength without harshness —
surely, surely the old Spanish painter must have known
redeeming love, since nothing less could have lent him
such inspiration for this work. Standing before it we
are quite tolerant (for the moment) of the image and
picture worship of the illiterate papist.

Wandering amongst the English pictures, and unable
to restrain some ejaculations of delight, we hear at our
elbow:

"Oh, these are nothing! You should come across the
water to see what we can do. We do not send *our best*
pictures to America!" Thus, pompous, self-complacent
John Bull. What an amusing contrast to the modest
Russian who, when told, "Your country has made a
magnificent display," replied: "No finer than the other
nations, although we brought the best we had!"

Signor Castellani's collection of majolicas, made by the
Arabs in Sicily, from the year 1200 to 1600, is a most
unique and interesting subject of study.

Also Raphael's ware, from the 15th to the end of the
16th century; the signor's gems, and mirrors, and toilet
articles, too, from Ninevah and Persepolis, the corrosion
and verdigris of ages testifying to their genuineness.
Also the marble busts of many long-forgotten great ones
of earth. It is probably gross ignorance, but we can
not affect admiration for these broken-nosed worthies.

A lively curiosity and mirth are the only emotions they excite in our benighted minds.

Here is the head, at least a large fraction of it, of Euripides, a tragic poet of Athens, born in Salamis 480 B. C. And here one of Tiberius, third emperor of Rome, born 42 B. C., died A. D. 37—found in Naples. Here, the Greek poetess Sappho, who lived more than half a thousand years before Christ, and there an Apollo, together with various other gods and goddesses of ancient Grecian story. But now these marble men and women revenge themselves for our unseemly levity. Spite of knocked-off chins and broken lips they seem to thunder, "You puny scions of a degenerate race, you should know all of history, and poetry, and mythology, since time began, before you prate of *us!*" We rally from this withering rebuke, to perpetrate a weak joke about their bilious cast of countenance, but are eclipsed by their nineteen centuries of stony calm, and, hiding our diminished heads, pass on.

John's Letter.

• • • ——

DEAR MOTHER, you will wonder what luck abroad I
find ;
My work is quite congenial, and the boss is very
kind.
But I 've been awful home-sick, I do n't mind telling
you.
Especially at night-fall, I was desperately blue.
I missed the pleasant home scenes where I was wont
to be,
Where I knew every body, and every one knew me ;
Where every living creature for my fortunes seemed
to care,
From the little yearling heifer to the stumbling old
gray mare.

So I formed a reckless habit of wand'ring through
the streets,
But a fellow is most lonesome in the biggest crowd
he meets !

The windows looked inviting, and through them I
    could see
Such friendly groups of people in social revelry!
Could hear the click of glasses, the joke and snatch
    of song,
And I grew morose and bitter, left outside every
    throng.
One night, when strangely moody, and full of
    thoughts of gloom,
My foot was on the threshold of Howard's billiard
    room,

When suddenly I started: a stranger said to me,
" Excuse me, friend, but do you seek pleasant com-
    pany?
We have an entertainment up at the Rooms to-
    night,
If you 'll go with me thither, I shall be happy quite."
Mother, a strain of music from over Heaven's wall,
I think would not be sweeter, than was that simple
    call :
For you a woman, can not guess how we poor boys
    fare,
Cast on a city's current, with not a soul to care.

The heart-ache and the longing just for a friendly
    tone !
(Perhaps it is n't manly such childishness to own),

I have n't much experience, and may be pretty
    green.
But being quite observant, I know what some things
    mean.
The snares we 've vaguely dreamed of, are not a
    myth, be sure :
Saloons at every corner, and gambling hells allure !
Gay trappings lend enticement to every vice and
    sin,
And I 've beheld that many are they who go therein.

But I 'm digressing sadly. My new friend led the
    way
Where hung illuminated, a sign " Y. M. C. A.! "
That night was my salvation ; for, mother, there and
    then
Society was offered with healthy, high-toned men.
Do n't think I 'm growing priggish : it is n't senti-
    ment,
But I believe an angel, that night, the stranger sent.
And do n't forget, in praying each day while I am
    gone,
To bless the Association, and your devoted John.

Christ Our Attraction.

...

Far on the plains of Texas,
  There blooms a little flower,
Which ever, through all changes
  Of sunshine, or of shower,
Through calm, or stormy tempest,
  Its leaves it putteth forth,
Unmoved by wind or weather,
  Steadfastly toward the North.

O, vacillating Christian,
  Torn by adversity,
Perchance an admonition
  Is hidden here for thee.
Learning from this mute teacher,
  The little Compass-flower,
Toward Christ, in joy or trial,
  Lean thou in every hour.

A traveler, in straying
  For years the wild world o'er,

A small, magnetic needle
  Safe in his bosom bore.
Strange lands, and waste of waters
  His soul could not dismay,
For through all devious wanderings,
  His true steel points the way.

So thou, O doubting Christian,
  Tossed on life's angry sea,
Shall never lose thy bearings,
  If Christ thy magnet be.
Grave dangers may encompass,
  Perils and grief o'erwhelm :
The harbor is assured thee,
  With Jesus at the helm.

In his lone watch, a sailor
  Was never once misled
By all the constellations
  That flamed above his head :
For, in the northern heavens
  One single light he knew,
And steered by that fair beacon,
  The pole-star, tried and true.

O, weak, half-hearted Christian,
  Loving the world too well.
Do myriad sweet allurements

Seek in thy soul to dwell ?
Fix thou thy roving vision
   Where in the heavens afar,
With never-fading glory,
   Shineth dear Bethlehem's star.

A ship, on troubled waters
   Tossed like an infant's toy,
Cared not for wrathful billow,
   In her coquettish joy.
She only rocked more lightly
   As storms went roaring past,
For staunch, and strong, and faithful
   The anchor held her fast.

And though thou seemest, Christian,
   The sport of time or chance,
Their impotent endeavors
   Shall but thy joys enhance;
Thou need'st not strive, nor wrestle,
   But laugh at every shock,
So long as thou art anchored
   In Christ, the living Rock.

Grandfather's House.

...

FRIDAY morning at school. Tramp, tramp, tramp came the young feet by hundreds up the stairs. A heterogeneous procession, of all classes and colors and conditions, past the task-mistress they file. Grim and still as a statue, save for the "eyes all round her head," she notes each lass and laddie, nice and winning, or rough and forbidding, and sees in each as Angelo saw, in the uncouth block of marble, an angel (sometimes awfully fast-prisoned indeed,) that she is sent to liberate. One little man halts to smuggle into her hands a pear. And what a pear! It must be wax! No: only the great artist could mold and color this, through his subtle chemists, sun and air and earth's juices. What a mammoth it is, and what a brilliant cheek it has! But how could the tooth of a child forbear to test this piece of perfection? Who knows what struggle and what victory transpired on the way to school, before this prince of pears could be laid on the teacher's shrine? Or was it a free-will thank-offering, the reason of which Johnnie knows, and she knows, and that is enough! Any way it is much too lovely and luscious to be devoured by any commonplace mortal. "Take it to Bessie's grandfather," suggests a good fairy, and so we did.

Close by the head-waters of the Susquehanna, the little basin that incloses Otsego lake holds also the hill-girt village of Cherry Valley,—

> "Somewhat back from the village street
> Stands the old-fashioned country-seat,"

that one would think Longfellow must have had in view when he wrote "the Old Clock on the Stairs;" and on Saturday, for the sake of a revered kinsman of ninety-one years, we found ourselves riding up the maple and willow avenue that leads to this "old-fashioned country-seat" known as Willow Hill. The quaint old mansion, built in English style; its atmosphere of by-gones; its ancient furnishings just as they were forty-seven years ago, all redolent of the associations of that long period; its courtly little formalities, its prodigal hospitality,—all unrolled themselves before us like a dream of departed days. No wonder that grandchildren and great-grandchildren succumb to the subtile fascination of the place, and hasten from near and far the moment vacation emancipates from school or business. Bric-a-brac hunters and the victims of the last fashionable craze for old things would go wild with delight in this house: over its window draperies of scarlet and amber brocatel, edged with funny, stiff little tasseled fringes, toned down with embroidered muslin beneath, and the whole depending from a cornice, scarce tarnished by a half century of service; its oddly carved chairs and tables, its imposing bed-hangings and solemn old clocks; its seven different sets and remnants of fine old china; and would pay fabulous sums, perhaps, for somebody else's grandfather's spinning-wheel and things, only to fling them aside for the next popular folly; but the present possessors of these household gods value them most for the memories which link them with their past.

But what impresses a stranger is the exquisite tenderness and veneration manifested by all the young people for Grandfather. It was a thing of such spontaneity and naturalness, of such graceful unconsciousness, that in these days, when it seems as if the bump of reverence had caved in on the head of Young America, it was most unique and beautiful. Grandfather's eye is still bright and his step tolerably firm, but his sense of hearing is a trifle dulled. With instinctive refinement he never asked what was being talked about. But a young girl, good as she was high-bred and beautiful, would attentively listen to what the new-comers said, and then with her arm over the patriarch's shoulder, in a high, sweet clear key, would begin — "Grandfather, she says." —and so rehearse the whole story. Or, if she sat apart from him, and the narrator nearer, she would say, "Will you please tell it so Grandfather will hear? *He'd* like that." So with the young gentlemen. There was the utmost deference and care, with perfect unaffectedness, that the dear old man should follow the conversation. When the boys, grand young fellows of twenty-five or so, waxed warm in discussion, Grandfather was referee and umpire, and his decision was accepted as final. I have never seen one of his great age who was so thoroughly abreast of the times in matters religious, social and political—due both to his own remarkably preserved mental and bodily vision, and to the loving companionship of children and grandchildren, and no end of ever welcome visitors. Even in the New York walking match he had his preference as to who should win.

On Sunday when apprised that the horses wait, we whisper to our senior traveling companion hither, "Why, this is n't the carriage that came for us to the station," and are told, *sotto voce*, "O no, this is another relic: the identical vehicle that fifty years ago used to bring the family to visit Massachusetts and Connecticut cousins. I remember it well, long before the days of steam and rail." As near as we can guess, it is the early style of the ponderous English barouche. Every vestige of color gone from the upholsterings, but its substantial comfort gives promise still, like the Deacon's

> " Wonderful one hoss shay,
> To run a hundred years to a day."

It only wants a tongue to tell famous tales of its pristine glory, when it gathered to its embrasure the happy family and with hampers of provisions for two or three days of gypsy life stored in its cavernous depths, it howled away from the Empire State home to old New England, over mountains and valleys and streams, until its welcome burden was deposited at the ancestral Connecticut farm.

Any other than the dignified high-church Episcopal service of that day in the village sanctuary, would have been out of harmony with the spirit of the place and time. Then there was the great Sunday dinner, when the table was resplendent in its heir-loom of gorgeous old pink and gold china, and joyful with the faces of four generations around the ample board, who coming to church from a radius of six miles, stop to dinner with father. That venerable man in the midst of his children's children made one think of the "righteous that shall grow like the cedar in Lebanon, and shall bring forth fruit in old age." The very domestics, tried and faithful, some of them with eighteen years of service, beam kindly on the scene, and the green parrot in the conservatory looks through the window and screams, "Father, father," with a comical air of interest and appreciation. Something of old school etiquette clings to the customs of the household. Always when summoned to the living-room, the family assemble in the upper hall,— which, curiously enough, is the favorite living-room, with its spacious proportions, its couches and rugs and invalid chairs and portraits with queer customs of former times — and here Grandfather gives his arm to some young lady, the young gentlemen take charge of the oldest ladies. Flossie crooks her dimpled elbow to Auntie, and we descend in some state. Arrived at the table, if Grandfather's partner is not versed in the ways of the house, Flossie fastens his napkin around his neck, likely as not bestows a kiss or love pat, and slips to her seat by the time the aged head is bent to ask the blessing. Presently all is activity, and we are so busy in appropriating the bounties of sheep-cote and duck-pond and harvest-field, and in following the flashes of repartee and humor that sparkle all about, that a fair, square, comprehensive stare has hardly been given to the scene; when lo! in a moment's lull, we spy — promoted to honor at the top of the center fruit-dish — *Johnnie's pear!* When duly admired, the unit is divided — (that is the pedagogic phrase) into as many fractions as there are mouths around the board, for Grandfather all his life has practiced sharing his good things with other people. When next week in school the fate of the big pear is related, Johnnie Richmond's bonnie brown eyes are luminous as stars, and the wee pale face turns red as his hair, as it drops on his desk in pleased confusion; under cover of which the teacher insinuates an " Oral Lesson" on the duty and beauty of devotion to age and respect to superiors. Pills of moral instruction must be sugar-coated with narrative. "Sowing on rock" you feel when contemplating the motley audience, where one may be as high-minded and pure in thought as he is neat in person — not always the case : and another, to whom has been preached vainly the beneficent gospel of soap and water, is more unkempt and chaotic within than without; and where the many are prone to acknowledge no authority higher than their own — any thing but sweet — wills; and to whom the words, "in honor, preferring one another," are vague and meaningless. But you take heart again when kindly reminded that "even rock disintegrates" with the lapse of time, and in the strange evolutions of nature that which is inanimate and inorganic changes into the animate and organic ; so who knows but that the morally weakest lambkin in the fold may catch a glimpse of "whatsoever things are lovely," the "stony ground where there is not much depth of earth " may unconsciously get a seed into its ungenial bosom that shall one day yield fruitage of at least thirty-fold ? (Michael Angelo's angel certainly there.)

The wall of one side of the lower hall of Grandfather's house is one continuous painting, and the opposite wall is a companion scene, undisturbed by frescoer or paperhanger now for forty-seven years. They seem to be Greek or Roman architectural ruins that are represented ; for here are elaborate Corinthian columns and simpler Doric pillars, together with such vegetation as is found in the Orient, and seas where lazy barges lie, and foreign-habited figures on the shore.

The house stands on historic ground. Here the fam-

17

ily of Col. Wells, of e'even persons, one only escaping,
were murdered by the Indians at the time of the Cherry
Valley massacre in 1778. The town, then the first white
settlement west of Albany, rendered weak by the absence
of its men in the War of Independence, was easily betrayed by a tory named Butler into the hands of the
celebrated Seneca half-breed, Joseph Brant. On the
side-hill in the rear of Grandfather's house, there was
then (as now) a tiny house where lived the Clydes, a family
of Scotch Covenanters. Mrs. Clyde saw the Indians coming over the wooded mountain, and, seizing her baby, ran
into the forest, crawled into a hollow log, and stuffed
her apron into the baby's mouth. Thus she escaped,
although the butt end of Brant's gun trailed over her
log. The rest of her family were murdered. Next, the
savages came to the Wells place. Jane Wells, a beautiful
girl of eighteen, fled a few steps to where now stands
the well-house, and was overtaken by Brant. On her
knees she begged piteously for her life, and the savage
for a moment seemed to waver, but presently drew his
scalping-knife and made an end of her petition. The
night came on, cold and stormy. A little girl of twelve,
clad in a frock of "calamink" (colonial, "calamanco"—
Webster,) escaping with her brother of four, hid under her
petticoat, was discovered and driven with other captives
to the Indian encampment. As the scouts came in, she
had the horror of seeing one redskin hold up for admiration a very beautiful scalp, which he was cleaning from

gore by drawing it through his fingers. She was now
tortured with the conviction that her mother was murdered, supposing no other woman in the village had hair
of that color and extraordinary length. But it was the
scalp of poor Jane Wells, and the little girl and brother
and mother were afterwards safely restored to each other.
Perhaps the child's senses were sharpened by terror and
by the hope of escape, for she saw through the disguise
of one of her captors, and knew him for a white man
who had worked for her father. When the camp was
still for the night, she crept cautiously to him, and im-
plored him to help her and her little brother to escape.
He feigned ignorance, but she adjured him, by the bread
he had eaten at her father's table and the kindness he
had received at the same hands, that he should aid them
in one desperate chance for life, and he finally con-
sented. Another tale is told of a woman and four children, who escaped by hiding under the snow among some
logs.

Last year was the one hundredth anniversary of this
massacre, and the citizens determined to call home the
sons and daughters of the town, and celebrate it by un-
veiling a statue to the fallen soldiers of the late war, and
by public speeches, dinner and other demonstrations.
Here at Willow Hill, the descendants of the one Wells
that escaped were to be guests, and a consultation was
held as to what should be the character of the home
celebration : whether it should be made a doleful or a

cheerful occasion. Learning, by a little strategy, that
the latter would best please their visitors, and well knowing the love of farce and fun in at least one of the expected party, they planned accordingly. Old and young
equipped themselves as first-class warriors of the Mohawk
and Seneca complexion. Tomahawks and scalping-
knives, blankets, wampum, war-paint and feathers made
them sufficiently hideous. Then, when the carriage had
been sent to the station, they disposed themselves in ambush amongst the shrubbery and behind the trees of the
yard and avenue. Soon as the horses were seen returning,—

"O, the wild charge they made!"

With the most approved war-whoops and much extrava-
gant brandishing of steel, our mock Indians welcomed
to Willow Hill the descendants of its first proprietor,
and, such was their delight at this novel reception, that
they compelled the whole scene to be re-enacted for them
later in the day.

It is useless to try to describe the charms of this old
place,—the rollicking, riotous, luxuriance of its great
orchards and gardens: its farm-house hard by: and a
dairy, with a herd of forty handsome Jerseys and Dur-
hams, one of which cost four hundred dollars, and all of
which furnish the so-called "gilt-edged" butter for the
metropolis.

Seen from the balcony, what grotesque pictures the

moonlight makes all down the valley.—what fantastic tricks the imagination plays! This is the fortress of some old feudal lord. The ridge of mountain in the rear is the castle wall. The narrow, deep brook below is the moat; and the odd, rustic arch across it, in the right foreground, is the draw-bridge. The old man's sanctum is the dungeon-keep. The countless comers and goers of the household are the knights and ladies. The men-servants and the maid-servants are the stanch " retainers." But the scene shifts. Weird and uncanny in the moonlight, on the hills and in the valley to the left, we see the hop-poles stacked conically for the season, just like a straggling camp of brown tents, that need only curling smoke from their tops to stimulate with startling effect the wigwams of the aborigines. Ugh! We are chilled with superstitious thrill, as if the crafty red men were skulking in the shadows, and hastily we descend to the light and cheer of the stately old parlor.

Here of a Sunday evening, a new and sweeter significance the old hymns seemed to have, sung by extreme age, middle life, youth and childhood; with Bessie tinkling an accompaniment out of the antique little piano; Ned's face blown out of its grave, fine cast, by his flute; Flossie, bewitching rosebud of a girl, near enough to cover her beloved Grandfather's hand as it rests on the arm of his chair, with her own warm little palm; and the sweet old face of Grandmother haloed with a muslin

frill. looking down from the wall,—we trust looking
down from Paradise.

But on another night, we found that age has its mirth-
ful as well as serious moods.   For at a family frolic at
the old man's son's, a half a mile distant, where stringed
instruments led by the inspiring violin provoked dancing and general jollity, this veteran of ninety-one, with
a little coaxing, showed the young folks how they " took
steps" in days of lang syne.   No languid walking
through the figures, but with pet Flossie for his partner
ninety-one and seventeen capped the climax as the most
"stunning" couple on the floor.   Grandfather is a
capital story-teller, too.   In the war of 1812, he was a
commissary of subsistence for the soldiers.   Later he
made the first calico prints ever manufactured in this
country.   Explained how, when a boy of twelve, he
watched an old woman in Suffield, Ct., spin yarn from
a spindle, and gathering ideas from her, in time digested
and matured them until they took shape in his own
memory.   The story of his madder dyes, and block-
prints, the cleaning of raw cotton from the seeds before
the invention of the gin,—were full of interest and instruction.   He sent the first cheese that ever went from
this country to England.   Grandfather whiled away for
us many delightful hours with tales of other days.
Willow Hill can need no tribute from our humble quill,
since its praises were more fitly told some years ago by
an earlier guest.—Mrs. H. B. Stowe.

And now vacation wanes. Sadness settles on the old house as the girls pack for Vassar, the boys to return to the harness of business and college life, and the guests to their home vocations. And when next we see dear venerable Grandfather, it may be no longer in the flesh, but where the spirit in Elysian fields has found the fountain of immortal youth.

1879.

A Word for the Pagan.

— • • • —

I DREAMED a sad and troubled dream.
  On waters wide I sailed,
For days and days, till overhead
  The constellations paled,
And stars unknown to our lone way
  Their lambent lustre lent :
The Southern Cross I saw, and knew
  We left the Occident.

And still we sailed : Pacific's wave
  Grew warm beneath our prow,
And phosphorescent insect fire
  Played, sparkling round the bow :
I sniffed Molucca's groves of spice :
  And still our course was bent
Toward lands that seem almost a myth—
  The fabled Orient.

At last we gained far India's shore,
  And up her sacred stream,

Strange tropic scenes on either hand.
   We floated in my dream:
Tall plumy palms and banyan trees
   Their pennons green unfurled.
In Brahmapootra's wondrous vales—
   The garden of the world.

And here the Deccan's bosom bore
   Golconda's treasures rare :
And gorgeous flowers, unknown before
   Bloomed marvelously fair:
From earliest ages coveted
   By nations of the West.
Yet, 'mid her lavish opulence,
   Sad India sits unblest :

For woman is a thing accursed :
   Dark-browed and dusky-eyed,
I saw her at her idol shrines,
   And Ganges' wave beside :
The very babe upon her breast,
   In superstition's zeal,
She flung to hungry crocodiles,
   As if her heart were steel.

I saw the martyred myriads
   Of mothers, anguish riven,
In nameless rites idolatrous,

Seek thus to purchase heaven:
Through prison-like Zenana walls
    Came woman's plaintive cry,
Till all the perfumed Indian air
    Echoed her misery.

O, Christian woman, bending low
    And late o'er fiction's page!
Can that imagined, sickly woe
    Thy sympathies engage,
While tragedies unknown, unsung
    By histrionic art,
Crush all the life and sweetness from
    Thy Hindoo sister's heart?

Rise, O thou highly favored one,
    And from thy hoarded pelf
Give lavishly! remembering
    That Jesus gave Himself:
And then in holy covenant
    Thy Christian vows renew,
And ask obediently: "Lord,
    What wilt Thou have me do?"

My Work.

∙∙∙　—

ONCE, when I was a school girl,
　I had a dream of fame :
I longed to be a painter,
　And win a deathless name.
And so I studied fondly
　The lives of artists through,
Until the dreaming student
　A wild enthusiast grew.

Friends, at the childish folly
　Laughed, as at last do I :
But *then* I vowed sincerely
　I 'd do it, or I 'd die —
So many a midnight found me
　Worshiping at the shrine
Of old Italian Masters,
　Whose genius seemed divine.

Sometimes I kept the vigil
　Till morn broke, soft and dewy.

Poring o'er lives of Raphael,
  Titian, or Cimabué;
And thus, in stealthy fragments,
  I gleaned the witching story
Of all the Artist heroes
  Renowned in olden glory.

I knew the tale of Guido,
  And Michael Angelo,
Of Leonardo da Vinci,
  And great Correggio.
The history of ancient
  And modern Art as well,
Was to my high wrought fancy
  Sweeter than tongue can tell.

Turner, and Church, and Landseer,
  Rosa Bonhenr, Doré;
Why should not I win laurels
  Of fame as well as they?
And so the wild chimera
  Impossible, as sweet,
With youth's untamed ambition,
  I chased with eager feet.

Poor? Yes indeed I knew it,
  Artists were *always* poor!
But all Golconda's treasure

Could not my heart allure,
And poverty was *welcome*,
Though cruel as the grave,
And sharp and sore and grinding —
I'd be her abject slave,—

If after life's long struggle,
In dying, I might claim
By reason of *one picture*
Right to a deathless name,
So, fostering wildest fancies—
Doomed to expire full soon,
My little, weak, child-fingers
Filled many a brave cartoon.

I burlesqued gouty grandpas,
And every neighbor's baby,
Till much astonished mothers
Judged me a genius—maybe!
At boarding school I frescoed
My chamber walls so bare,
And then did penance roundly
On bread and water fare.

Years passed—an earnest woman
The school girl grew at length,
But that absorbing passion
But strengthened with my strength.

And then — Unfathomed Wisdom
  Looked on my zeal and pride,
And whispering — "Child, aim higher,"
  Reversed my life's whole tide.

A short, sharp strife — then humbly
  I kissed the Hand divine,
And brokenly made answer :
  " Lord, not my will but Thine."
Now, to a public school-room
  My earthly mission led,
With coward soul a-tremble,
  And half uncertain tread.

Up spake a voice in chiding,
  " It is the task you sought,
And nowhere for the Master
  Can grander work be wrought.

" Narrow, obscure, unvalued,
  Except as God shall know,
The *school-room* hence becometh
  Your Artist studio,
Immortal *minds* your canvas,
  And deathless *souls* as well :
Here paint ! but know you 're painting
  For heaven — or for hell.

The cross of Christ your easel,
　　There hallow each design ;
Your palette and its colors
　　Draw from the Book divine,
And for *unfading* pigments
　　Let *Truth* your background be.
Then, *Principles of Virtue*
　　Lay on religiously.

" The Science, and the Learning,
　　And Art of all the schools,
Within your power of using,
　　Shall further be your tools.
Materials from all ages
　　Choose ye with loving pains,
Then " mix," with dextrous judgment,
　　As Reynolds did — " *with brains.*"

" You sighed to leave one picture
　　Worthy to outlive thee.
Here you shall paint a *thousand*
　　For immortality."

The speaker ceased — but left behind
　　An influence sweet and pure,
Which permeated all my toils,
　　And shall while toils endure.
No longer in half doubting mood

I turn me to my task,
Heaven's blessing, and a conscience clean,
  The only boon I ask.
The public may depreciate,
  Belittle, and abuse,
Who chooses *teaching* for her work,
  Grim poverty must choose.
Deliberately must count the cost,
  Then, if she can, elect
That parents, school-boards, officers
  Shall analyze, dissect —

That moneyed kings shall vote her worth
  A kitchen scullion's pay !
Who gives the *best years of her life*
  All lavishly away,
To mould *their children*, that she may
  In vast Eternity,
Say, "Here am I, thy servant, Lord,
  With them thou gavest me."

Sunday School Teaching

FOR THE YOUNGER SCHOLARS.

— • • • —

SIR PHILIP SYDNEY once said to a poet : " Look into your own heart, and write." So perhaps the best exordium that can be made in an essay on Teaching is, Look into your own heart, and teach !

Teaching of the Infant Class is the exalted duty assigned us to-day, and if we let fall any hint that is worth your remembrance, please attribute it to the Superintendent of Trinity Sunday School, to whose kind suggestions we are indebted for the thoughts we have now to offer.

We say *exalted* duty, not only because public sentiment is coming to demand the best devotion, the largest talent and the widest culture for primary learners, both secular and religious, but because our own convictions acknowledge the fitness of this demand. The half-grown child has learned to help himself and exercise his own efforts. He *begins* to have some judgment and discrimination in regard to the instruction afforded him, may accept or reject as his own sense of truth shall ap-

18

prove or disprove; but the *little* child has *none* of this elective power in regard to morals and religion; his little mind is *only receptive,* can not tell wheat from chaff, nor truth from error. Therefore, give the little ones the *best* teachers.

The instruction of the Infant Class is Primary in two senses. First, it is of *primary importance.* It is a well-known fact, that, during the first ten years of life, the mind learns more than during any other ten years of its existence; and the knowledge acquired during these first ten years has far greater influence upon character and destiny, than that acquired in any after period. Voltaire said that if he could have the whole control of any child during its first *fire* years, he would so un-alterably fix its principles that no after influence should counteract his work! Who knows but that his own in-fidel death was attributable to his *very early* indoctrina-tion into the sceptical literature of the day? How im-portant, then, that the little ones have the *best* teachers!

Again, the instruction of the Infant Class is primary, inasmuch as it is *preparatory* for mature instruction, and it begins at the first and lowest stage of mental de-velopment. The mind upon which the teacher is now to act is pure, innocent and simple.—a fair, clean page from the hand of its Great Author. What and how shall the teacher write on this white, unsullied page? "*Love first,* and then you may do what you will!" says Augustine.

Consecration, then, seems the first and most imperative requisite in the teacher ; — supreme love to God, and
in a large degree that genius for " maternity of souls,"
as some one has said, that characterizes many noble
Christian women. With such consecration, the teacher
may then survey her field. She sees several score of
restless, lively, inquisitive little "demi-semi-quavers" of
humanity : — the dainty pets from homes of affluence
and luxury, and the children of humble poverty, in garments scant and coarse ; and in *every* one she recognizes
a possible jewel for the Master, just as the sculptor, in
the rough, unchiseled stone, sees an angel that *he* is
sent to liberate. " How shall I teach these young im-
mortals," asks the teacher, " A, B, C of sacred things?
How lead these tottering lambs to the Good Shepherd ? "
And so, second only to consecration, we would write

Adaptation, as an important requisite. The teacher
must be able to place herself in the condition of her little learners. She must go back in memory, and try to
recall the weakness and dimness of her own mental
dawn, and the small sphere of thought of her own in-
fantile days.

She must cultivate her imagination, and her sympathetic emotions, and *so* learn to fit her instructions to
the capacity of her pupils. She need not be *childish*,
nor in any sense let herself down, in thus identifying
herself with the feelings and sentiments of her little
flock ; but she must needs be *childlike*, and present her

thoughts in language that shall be characterized by
severe simplicity. We are reminded of a good minister,
who began his address to a Sabbath School in this wise :
" My little children, the Bible is *eminently a didactic
book!*" The teacher who has tact and the instinct of
adaptation will not talk in that style to "*little children.*" She will remember that the child's vocabulary
is small : his intellect is small : his knowledge, his judgment, his ability to receive instruction, all are small, and
she must adapt herself to all these conditions.

But the grandest truth may be made level with the
capacities of the Infant Class, if the teacher has this
power of insight as to their needs, and of adaptability
to those needs : if she knows how to " put herself in
their place," and especially, if she habitually sits at the
feet of the Great Teacher, humble, simple, and teach-
able as a little child. By practice and association with
her charge, she will learn to be discriminating in child-
character. She will learn where to encourage and draw
out the sensitive and timid, where to restrain with firm-
ness and decision the over-bold, and where to arouse with
her own vigor and energy the dull and listless. All in her
class have many things in common : but just as no two
faces are exactly alike, so no two minds are alike : and
every child has some distinctive, individual trait, that
makes him quite unlike every other child. An intimate acquaintance with these traits, and a clear
understanding of each child's peculiarities, will greatly

aid the teacher in her power of adaptation, and wonderfully increase her faculty of communicating knowledge. If she thus carefully and keenly observes, and makes a separate study of human nature in each individual, (which she can do only when the class is numerically small, and her time largely at her own command,) she will be prevented from firing over their heads, or, in homely Western phrase, "the fodder will not be put too high in the rack for the lambs to reach." She will *constantly remember* that she is acting upon minds that are extremely limited, and that have but few ideas; and, by this constant remembrance, she will come to have a constantly augmenting power of transferring into these little minds what exists in her own. We insist, then, that this aptness to teach may be increased by cultivation and practice; but, it must be admitted that it is largely a gift also, and the true teacher, like the poet, is "born, not made."

Another important element of success is

Enthusiasm. The teacher must love her work. A man may dig a ditch, and a woman may sweep a floor without putting a *great* deal of enthusiasm into the act. But the teacher's work is too vital to admit of mere mechanical efforts. While she paints on the immortal canvas of mind, she must mix *her* colors, not "with brains," only, as did Sir Joshua Reynolds, but with *heart and soul.*

What thoughts can inspire her with this enthusiastic

love for her vocation ? We answer, a profound sense of her responsibility to God. There *are* moments when she will be oppressed and saddened and dismayed when she contemplates her task. But her courage will come again : she will exult, with the joy and gratitude of an unworthy vassal who has received some fadeless honor from his king. *Her* King has dared trust *her* to lay a moulding hand upon the plastic clay, that shall harden into marble with her imprint upon it.

She is shaping character for the future men and women that in these babes exist only as grand, though distant, possibilities. Neither will her influence stop here. But the truths she imparts, will, by these young disciples, be imparted one day to their children, and they in turn shall teach the same principles to the children of a yet later generation ; and she will thus be living, in her influence, long after the heart that felt and the brain that thought, have crumbled back to dust.

Here, then, in the fact of her responsibility, and in the inspiring thought of a pure and deathless influence, she may kindle the flame of a glowing enthusiasm in her work. Another needful qualification is

Versatility. The teacher must be able to give variety to the exercises. Maps and blackboards are necessities, and she may let individuals trace routes, or indicate localities, on the maps, and may herself make free use of the blackboard. Singing may be interspersed often, and frequent changes of position be allowed.

A long period of enforced quiet is an unreasonable demand on young children, and a thwarting of Nature's designs. She has made them frisky as colts, and frolicsome as kittens. The proportion of brain and nervous system is larger than the other bodily organs in early life, and the activity of childhood is involuntary as the breath. It is insufferably irksome for many adults to *sit still* for an hour; how much more so for the Infant Class!

Again, much depends upon the *manner* in which the teacher imparts, and she will need to study

Methods. Often she must employ the *Catechetical* style, since very little fixedness of thought can be expected of young children, and the youngest will only be able to respond in monosyllables.

Often she must introduce simple *Illustration and Figure.* For children get dim and erroneous notions about many things, where, with visible illustrations, they might get vivid and correct ideas at a glance. Power to simplify in this way will make her lessons attractive and easy to hold, and will be a source of strength. She may also employ

Anecdote to point her instructions. Who does not know a child's delight in stories, even in stale and ofttold tales? And often some little story will clinch the truth in a child's mind, since, by the law of association, his recollection of the story suggests the principle taught.

The teacher may also employ the *Descriptive* style. Let her make a word picture of her lesson, and then ask some child, in whom perhaps, language is larger than in the others, to rehearse the same scene.   Possibly she will find that he has a more attentive audience than herself! And it is a profitable exercise in teaching the child *exactness of statement.*   To these babes only a little can be taught at a time, but it is desirable that the lessons have continuity from Sunday to Sunday, and care must be taken that all the instruction be thoroughly evangelical, and pervaded by a spirit of reverence and sacredness.

Children are keen observers; and any thing about the teacher that distracts their minds from the lesson should be laid aside.   A story is told of a lady who labored in vain to secure the attention of *one* of her girls, until she divested her finger of a diamond ring.   Its fascinating glitter was fatal to the good she would do, and she had the good sense to omit it from her Sabbath toilet.

Visiting the children in their homes, friendly acquaintance and sympathy with their parents, are valuable auxiliaries to success.   By this means greater interest may be awakened, and better preparation secured for the lessons.   It takes time, but is a profitable investment of the time.

Not five minutes' walk from this place there stands a handsome pile of architecture; substantial, commodious and enduring, as brick and iron with the skill of man can make.   But some remember that long before a brick was laid, there were weary toilers and massive enginery busy under-ground, driving piles, day after day, week after week, *only* driving piles. Now and then, some curious passer-by paused a second to watch this work beneath the surface, and thoughtfully ponder its significance. In good time the superstructure rose steadily to completion, beautiful, secure and strong. So the Primary Teacher is building a foundation on which others, in the Intermediate and Adult Departments, are to erect a building; and the foundation, although not the most showy, *is* the most important part of the mental, as of the material, structure. Early impressions *are the most lasting*, early instructions *most* certain, in their results.

Teaching of the Infant Class may seem to some an insignificant work. Like the patient delver in a coal-mine, like the pearl diver in Indian seas, the teacher is comparatively out of sight, working beneath the surface unobserved, unappreciated of men. But in days to come, when the tempest of life begins to thicken about these little ones, her words shall fructify at last, in warmth and comfort and salvation; her precept and example shall send them searching with eager, aching hearts for the Pearl of great price; her labor shall not be in vain in the Lord.

Lang Syne.

Written by request for Mr. Barrows' Farewell Reception.

— • • • —

A CHEERLY soun' is in the air,
  The dear auld Tutor's name!
It echoes blithely everywhere,
  His bairnies calling hame,
      Now ilka chiel wi' lusty lung
        Shout auld lang syne!
      Auld voices blending wi' the young
        In auld lang syne.

That kindly, wise, paternal rule
  There willna one forget
Who's kenned the World's severer school,
  Where sterner tasks are set.
      Then prithee, tho' your lips have quaffed
        Life's sweet and bitter wine,
      Where found they ever purer draught
        Than joys of auld lang syne?

Ye 've journeyed lang, ye laddies braw,
  And lassies once sae fair,
Till now some tell-tale flecks of snaw
  Glint in your own bright hair;
      While Maister's cheek is ruddy still
        Wi' bonnie, wintry bloom,
      Tho' mony a bairn 's by Heaven's will,
        Paled early for the tomb.

Ah, when our senses Death shall steal,
  May we the summons dread
As little as a tired chiel
  Its welcome trundle-bed;
      And taught and teacher gather yon,
        Where joys ne'er decline,
      And all regretful thochts are gone
        For auld lang syne.

1885.

A Glance at the Class Book.

— ••• —

In a little Roman province, centuries ago,
While the silent stars kept vigil over all below,
There was born an infant, of a maiden mother mild,
And a humble manger cradled Him, the Holy Child.

Wondrous living, wondrous dying, He, the God-
        man, showed :
Heaven its crowning gift to mortals thus in Him
        bestowed.
But e'er that last night of horrors lowered, with its
        gloom,
I recall Him, with His brethren, in "the upper
        room."

And I fancy His disciples listened, with hushed
        breath,
To the mournful words He uttered of His coming
        death ;

And their hearts were strangely heavy, for they
      could not know
That to us a pledge of ransom was His weight of
      woe.

Thus, through the slow-marching ages,
    Down, down to the present time,
The members of that upper chamber
    Hold memories sweet and sublime,
And methinks there are still apartments,
    And still there are privileged walls,
Where the voice of the Saviour echoes,
    Where the foot of the Master falls.

We see Him not in the door-way :
    For our Heavenly Guest no chair
We set in the midst, yet somehow
    We know that Jesus is there :
We hear no words benignant :
    We look not into His face :
Yet, touched with an awe, we whisper,
    " This is a heavenly place."

'T is the olden Methodist class-room —
    Term of significance sweet :
To remember its joys exalted,
    Dear comrades, to-night we meet.

We meet to rehearse His mercies,
 And the tale of the past unfold.
And give to the Lord the glory,
 For to-night we are *ten years old!*

All unrevealed lay the future,
 Its secrets we did not know,
When first, in an "upper chamber,"
 We gathered ten years ago ;
And some that we met that evening,
 Our fairest and tenderest flowers,
By the Gardener's hand are transplanted
 To more genial and heavenly bowers.

One tender bud there was gathered,
 The child of many a prayer ;
But we know in the Saviour's bosom
 He blossoms divinely fair ;
Too cold our soil for his culture,
 Too bitter the storms that destroy,
In Elysian fields we shall find him,
 Our beautiful, bright Willie boy.

And sweet Maggie Kenyon's red roses
 Grew pale and pure as the snow,
And our hearts were smitten with sorrow
 When we knew that Maggie must go ;

"She will be at *home* up in heaven."
    The faithful class-leader said ;
Can he say it as truly, O sister,
    O brother, when you, too, are dead ?

And dear little Nettie Allen,
    I think, over heaven's high walls,
Undrowned by the music of seraphs,
    She caught her dead mother's calls
And hastened with feet so eager,
    The darling, dutiful child,
To follow, wherever it led her,
    That summons, so winning and mild.

Brother Powell, the veteran hero,
    With his armor burnished and bright,
Fell out of the ranks all bravely,
    He having "fought a good fight."
Sister Justin, the dear, aged pilgrim,
    Awaiting permission to "come,"
Calm, patient and peaceful and saintly,
    All joyful her spirit went home.

Sister King, the fragile young mother,
    Like a bird on a bleak foreign strand,
She pined and drooped for a season,
    Then soared to the far spirit-land.

One more, Sister Buffum, has fallen :
But the long severed links of the chain,
We know, by-and-by, over yonder,
Shall be reunited again.

We have seen how many a dear one,
In the faith of our dear Lord has died !
We have launched full many another
On the matrimonial tide !
Like a Florentine piece of mosaic,
Our life, with its shrine and its shade,
So many and checkered the changes,
We have known in the last decade.

They seem to go filing past me,
These phantoms of by-gone years,
And I look in their vanished faces,
Through tender and fast flowing tears :
Some thorns have been mixed with the roses
Along the path we have trod ;
Some gems have slipped from our fingers,
Some flowers are under the sod.

They were treasures, lent for a little,
To lighten our toil and our pain :
And not very far in the future,
I know we shall have them again.

Ah, then, more joyfully backward
　We shall look on the path we 've trod,
As we number our treasures over,
　Up yon, in the kingdom of God.

19

The Twenty-first Anniversary

OF THE NORTH MAIN STREET CLASS OF TRINITY CHURCH.

. . .

WHAT ails us all?   When Methodists
    Their classes are forsaking?
Yet never fail to crowd the lists
    At every merry-making?

We 've time for kettle-drum, or call,
    Or any fun and frolic —
But speak of class — and faces all
    Grow long and melancholic!

We 've grown so dull, that many a class
    Takes a prolonged vacation —
Until, alas! it 's come to pass
    We 're near annihilation.

But Atwood's — never dry nor sere!
    It blooms and thrives perennial.
And once a year we 'll gather here
    Perhaps — until its centennial!

If not, we'll make the most of *this*,
　The twenty-first anniversary,
And celebrate the worth, the bliss
　Of class, the soul's kind nursery.

And when, at last, Beyond we've passed
　All peril of disaster,
We'll hope to meet, low at the feet
　Of Jesus, Lord and Master.

FRIENDLY WORDS.

TO THE MEMORY OF

Clara J. Loomis.

INSTRUCTOR, friend, your work is o'er,
  You who so lately walked our streets;
Your spirit, soon released, did soar
  To find above the heavenly seats.

Ah! who most intimate did know
  The love and patience of the years
In which you taught the mind to grow,
  Prepared its flight for better spheres?

Yours was the teacher's weary toil,
  To elevate the mind and soul,—
Sometimes a sluggish mind, a soil
  All full of weeds without control.

Ah! who can tell how much you've done
To Christianize and build the State?

A base of granite, well begun,
   You founded for the truly great.

You were a friend in friendship's needs,
   Sweet sympathy you freely lent,
Your joy was surely the meed
   Of joy which you to others sent.

We can not think your sojourn short,
   Although in mid-life borne away,
You have too many blessings brought,
   And sing redemption's song to-day.

IN MEMORIAM

Clara J. Loomis.

ONE more is added to the list
  Of households filled with anguish:
From home another loved one missed,
  Yet more sad hearts to languish.
But, friends, amid your grief be still;
Bow humbly to Our Father's will.

'T is he can heal the aching heart,
  All crushed, and sad, and lonely;
Can soften anguish, soothe the smart,
  And in his goodness, only,
Does he afflict the ones his love
Has given a hope of rest above.

He chastens whom he loves. Blest thought,
  That every pang that meets us
By loving hands is portioned out;

20

So, while this promise greets us
Of rest for those who love the Lord,
We trust, contented in his word.

While drinking of this bitter cup,
　　Know, Jesus, o'er her bending,
Bore in his arms her spirit up;
　　To heaven her steps were tending,
And she has reached a peaceful home,
Where sin and sorrow can not come.

Released from earthly toil and pain,
　　Her joyful voice is ringing
With angel bands, in glad refrain,
　　The Saviour's praises singing.
No sorrow clouds her radiant brow,
No pain, no suffering meets her now.

See, 'mid the ransomed throng in white,
　　The loved one you are mourning;
A harp of gold, a crown of light,
　　Her seraph form adorning.
Your household on this earthly shore
One less; in heaven, one angel more.

And when, your own life sojourn o'er,
　　Death's solemn summons meets you,

Her welcome to the shining shore
  Will be the first that greets you;
Love's severed chain rejoined in heaven,
Its links shall never more be riven.

N. G. J.

July 10, 1886.

In Memoriam.

Thou wert tired, and just stopped to rest
    By the way.
There broke o'er thee a radiance so blest,
    Only a ray
From God refracted,—
But earth could not restrain thee
Nor loving ones detain thee
From all the fullness of that life divine;
And thou,—the joy of entering in is thine
    To-day.

The flowers we love the best,
    They say,
Are first to wither,—ah, how blest
    Alway!
If but to Heaven transplanted,
And then so fondly cherished,
Thou hast not rudely perished,
But in soul-communion 'mong those radiant bowers
Art living still, a gladder life than ours
    To-day.

Springfield, 1886.   V. A. S.

www.ingramcontent.com/pod-product-compliance
Lightning Source LLC
Chambersburg PA
CBHW020855020726
47497CB00005B/1420